THROW CAUTION
TO THE WAVES

By Sarah Batsford Fraser

First published 2024

The characters in this book are entirely fictional, however, some of the events are inspired by the author's part in a real wild swimming group called the Broch Selkies of Burghead, as well as with a light-hearted 'coven' of 'sea witches' in Findhorn, both of Moray, Scotland. These hardy women take to the sea in all weathers, shrieking, laughing and worshiping the almighty ocean. The fictional locations of Brogie Bay and Findhoun are based on these two real areas in Moray, with name changes to allow for artistic licence.

ACKNOWLEDGEMENTS

Thank you to my inspiring friends – I'm lucky to know some strong, creative, hilarious women.

Huge appreciation to my family (especially Fraser, Lewis, Pearl, Connie, Chris and May) for always believing in my writing and loving me in all my weird and wonderful chapters of life. Thanks, mum, for that night you let me doodle with a pen in my babygrow when I should have been sleeping! I'm no different now, up all hours writing.

Thanks, Simon, for being a huge support and going through this whole process with me. You were my test reader, my sounding board, my cocktail partner and you even got in the sea with me on a gloomy, rainy day to get the authentic experience.

To us, to life…to dooking!

CHAPTER 1 - BRYDIE

B lue skies stretched on forever above Brogie Bay. Brydie examined the colour. Was it azure? Perhaps cobalt blue. She would look it up later. Brydie was an amateur jewellery maker and had started taking notice of colours around her. This new creative outlet had come after her fleeting passion for pottery, which was now no more than a smeared grey stain on her craft apron.

Brydie took a deep breath and closed her eyes. Her curly auburn hair danced in the cool spring breeze which tickled her face. The cold sand under her bottom kept her grounded while her mind floated off into weightless nothing. She opened her eyes again, focussing on the white froth of an incoming wave. *I am here, in this moment,* she told herself.

A seagull soared past, changing direction at speed as if it was weaving through invisible sky traffic. Brydie followed it with her gaze until it was no more than a white dot against the blue backdrop.

The long, curved stretch of beach – which ran from the east peninsula of Brogie past Rossy-isle beach and then ended at the other peninsula of Findhoun beach to the west – was practically empty, aside from a few dog walkers in the distance. Gentle barking sounds travelled over the undisturbed sandy landscape. Doug, Brydie's husband, was at work. Just thinking of that gave her a stab of guilt in her stomach. He worked so hard. He actually liked his career though.

Computing had been his life since school, so it was natural for him to move into a life of IT work. Brydie had no real concept of what Doug actually did on a daily basis, but she was envious of his purpose. At thirty-nine years old, she had hoped that by now some mythical creature or fairy godmother of sorts would have appeared in a blaze of white light to show her 'the way'. What was her purpose?

Brydie turned to runes and cards for answers on a regular basis but always felt frustrated at the vague messages of something true being just around the corner. *Where the hell is this corner?* she often wondered. *I've been around a thousand corners and not one has revealed my calling in life.*

A few years ago, she ventured into social care, thinking that maybe her nurturing personality could be harnessed and used to look after vulnerable adults. It was fine at first. She didn't mind wiping bums and walking around supermarkets with clients, trying to persuade them to buy nutritional food, but eventually 'the system' got to her. The complaints from clients' families about every last detail (stained bedding, not getting enough social opportunities, being put to bed too early so that staff members could go home at a reasonable hour...) coupled with being guilt-tripped into taking on unreasonable shifts at all hours of the day due to staff shortages got to her. She had less time to care about people, despite spending more time on the job. The moment it all turned dark was when a client was hospitalised with a really bad bout of vomiting and diarrhoea and the family of the client questioned Brydie's hygiene standards. Had they not seen her on her hands and knees with a bucket of bleachy water just hours before their sharp-worded email hit the boss's inbox? No! They hadn't, because they never bloody came to visit.

Her soul shrivelled into a dusty husk during her two years in the job until she spent full days wallowing in bed whenever she wasn't working. It was Doug who made the push for her to stop. He said he wanted 'his' Brydie back; the one who was always smiling, always creating trinkets or home decor and had a unique sparkle.

Six months had passed since Brydie chucked her job. She thought she would feel relieved and enjoy her freedom. All she felt was doom. Another failed job. The frustrating thing was she felt like someone with so much passion for life, but had no clue where to aim this passion when it came to careers.

Doug had two kids, aged ten and twelve. Brydie had known them for several years and always looked forward to them coming for weekends. It looked like babies weren't on the cards for her and Doug together. They'd been trying for three years. At first Brydie had trusted the universe that it would all happen at the right time, taking pregnancy vitamins religiously and meditating in front of a mood board filled with pictures of zen-like nurseries and models with blossoming pregnant bellies. The mood board now lived in the cupboard under the stairs, along with her withered hopes. Doctors were now thinking that she was in early menopause and had a severely diminished stock of eggs.

Brydie hugged her knees in tight as she sat on the sand watching the water edge ever closer. *You shouldn't be sitting on cold ground*, she thought in her granny's warning voice. *You'll get haemorrhoids.* A small smirk crept on Brydie's face to think of the huge bank of advice from her granny that was stored in her mind for moments like this. Granny always seemed so sure of her role in life. There never seemed to be a restless need for answers in her existence. It was a different time back when granny was young though. Just being married and keeping a nice home was enough of a purpose for many. Not that Brydie really excelled in that either. Cleaning was at the bottom of her 'to do' list every time. There was always some kind of art project or social plan commandeering her energy. *That's it*, she thought, tossing a perfectly round pebble across the sand, *I was born to be a wealthy socialite, like in The Great Gatsby. None of this 'lost cause job-hunting' was part of my destiny.* A light laugh tugged at her lips.

She sighed and examined the glossy water as it rested easily on the shore. The waves were relaxed today, no more than gentle licks at the sand, their hissing sounds soothing Brydie's weary mind. An idea poked at her annoyingly. *I want to swim*, she thought. *Is that totally crazy though? Have I officially lost the plot? What would someone think if they walked past and I'm in those waves in my undies?*

She tried to shrug off the temptation, yet it continued to poke at her. *Get in. Why not? Throw caution to the wind… or the waves! You used to do it as a kid without even thinking about it.*

Memories of dooking came flooding back like a rushing wave. For those who don't know, dooking is a Scottish term for a casual swim. It's what she'd grown up knowing. Summer holidays off school were all about sea and sand. Yet why had adulthood distanced her from that exhilarating pleasure?

Brydie rose to her feet, stretching out the stiff aches that came with sitting so long in one position. She looked left and right, searching for potential onlookers. The coast was clear. She began to laugh as she pulled off her knitted jumper, feeling the cool breeze prickle her skin with slight shocks. Next, she dropped her jeans to the sand, kicked off her trainers and tugged off her socks. She rubbed her slender arms in an embrace as goosebumps formed on the surface of her pale skin. *Am I really doing this?* There was no going back. You can't stand for very long on a beach in north Scotland in only a bra and pants before making a decision to either embrace the plunge or put your cosy layers back on. She started running small, light steps on the hard, wet sand, down to the water's edge and broke the barrier of sand and water with a yelp. She gasped as her feet plunged into seriously cold water. It was the month of May, but the water still thought it was winter. Further and further, she darted into the sea, jumping over small crashing waves and giggling like her younger self.

Before long she was thigh deep. She let out a shriek as an unexpected swell of water hit her private parts! *Ooh ya bugger.*

She took a few strides further out to waist depth then with a flutter of excitement and a racing heartbeat, she clasped her palms together and stuck them out like an arrow before plunging her shoulders right in and beginning to breaststroke. It was agony and euphoria all in one. Her skin cells were screaming *mayday mayday* as she kept moving to cope with the shock. After a couple of minutes, she noticed her skin was no longer sore, it was tingling, almost as if it was warm. It was the most bizarre sensation. She tapped the sand with her toe, feeling safe in the knowledge she could stand up and walk back to shore at any moment.

With her body now calm in the water her head had clarity and fear snuck in. *What am I doing out here on my own? What if a huge wave swept me out to sea? What if I fainted and drowned and there was no-one around to help?* Brydie took a deep breath in and examined her surroundings. As she exhaled, she let go of her worries. The only waves happening were the gentle murmurs which crashed on the sand. Where she was swimming was flat calm, like a vast mirror. Another deep breath and she was beginning to relax again. Looking out to the horizon she suddenly felt insignificant and free. The calm water looked silver from her viewpoint, reflecting cotton-white puffs of cloud back up at the sky. The silky, silver water stretched ahead for miles and miles, eventually meeting the hilly horizon of the Black Isle and the Highlands as they stretched further north. It was as if Brydie had never seen a horizon before. This new angle gave everything a whole new perspective. She was actually *inside* the horizon, in a way. Any frustration she harboured when she had been sitting on the sand was lost. Her anxiety must have floated away on the water because there were no fragments remaining.

She noticed a huge smile pulling at the corners of her lips. This felt insane, but unbelievably exciting. Brydie allowed herself to whisper the cliched words *I feel so alive.*

Just then, a black arrow-like slit cut through the water's surface up ahead. Brydie's heart quickened. She'd watched bottle nose dolphins from the harbour wall many times, but never had she been in the water *with* them. She clasped her hands together by her chin, as if in prayer, and held her breath. About 20 metres further out to sea, the dolphin stopped teasing and breached in a magnificent display, causing a satisfying splash and ripple as it dove back under. Brydie gasped. She was frozen to the spot, her toes sinking into the sandy seabed below.

Two other dolphins appeared, as if they had teleported from elsewhere, and the trio continued the performance like a well-rehearsed synchronised swimming team until they were so far into the distance Brydie could only make out small black flecks on the surface of the water.

She exhaled slowly and relaxed her shoulders. She began to notice her fingers feeling cold again and her dream-like giddy state cleared like a mist giving way and the sensible part of her recognised it was time to get out. She had no idea how long was safe to swim or what the temperature was. Better to play it safe. She turned towards the shore and began wading through the depths, feeling her muscles strain against the pressure.

As she trotted back up the sand in her drenched undies, a dog walker called out: "Are you mad?"

Brydie jumped. She hadn't even noticed another living being. She let out an awkward laugh. "I must be, yeah!"

She pulled on her clothes as shivers began to vibrate through her core. As crazy as this felt, Brydie knew this was only the beginning for her. This simply had to be recreated. She felt high as a seagull soaring in the breeze.

What would Doug think when she told him, because she absolutely would. Brydie couldn't keep any secrets, and this was way too exciting to withhold.

Life was going to get more interesting. She could feel it.

CHAPTER 2 - RAY

It was 6am on a spring morning, which in north-east Scotland, means there was the most beautiful, gentle dawn light. The sun was peering round the horizon, as if whispering to the landscape to wake up, not quite blasting its full beams just yet. This time of day was Ray's great love. She rose with the sun every morning, took a bag of supplies to the beach in front of her home and welcomed the new day.

This bag of supplies...let's just say, you wouldn't get it through customs. Among her flask of herbal tea, her small rug for meditating on and a floaty kimono jacket covered in beaded designs which she took on and off all day long, thanks to the everchanging Scottish climate, there was usually a loosely rolled joint or some homemade cannabis fudge.

Time, you see, was a luxury to Ray. She had retired – if you can retire from never having done very much – quite early at fifty-five and had used her inheritance money from both parents to buy the smallest, most adorable, beach-facing cottage you could ever imagine. It had just one bedroom and a small lounge with a log burner and a window looking onto the waves. Everything she could need. There were always jobs needing done in the place – a toilet that only flushed every third pee (if you had the knack to get it going), a bedroom door which was so warped it didn't shut properly, kitchen cupboards you had to hold onto while opening to avoid them collapsing at an angle on one hinge - but Ray had neither the funds or the motivation to worry too much about it. In Ray's mind there was nothing a piece of bohemian fabric dyed in vivid colours couldn't cover and enhance. She also had many, many, many picture frames on all the walls, partly to document her life as a traveller and partly to hide parts of the ancient cottage where the plaster had given up the ghost and left this world.

Any time guests popped into Ray's tiny palace, questions began to flow about the rock stars in photos on her walls.

"Oh, that's me with the band," Ray would reply nonchalantly, mid drag of a spliff. "Yeah, I dated the bassist for a few months and followed them on tour. I can't remember why we broke up now." She would drift off into a brain haze then emerge several minutes later as if there had been no pause in her story and say with a laugh something like: "Oh yes, I remember now. He caught me in bed with the manager and left me on a river boat in Berlin. I had to hitch hike my way back." She would smile as if she'd just regaled a lovely, happy tale that anyone could relate to.

One bright 6am, with her bag draped over her sloping, relaxed shoulder, Ray left the house, pulling the front door gently and shrugging with minimal effort to notice it had bounced off the frame and swung out an inch or so, open to the rest of the village. Anyone who fancied a nosey around the home of the happiest hippy in Brogie could quite freely wander in, if they so wished, but Ray was of the mindset that if the house wanted to be open, then open it should be – this was not the first time this had happened. Whatever.

After walking all of two minutes along the grassy path between her, open, house and the beach, Ray dropped her bag with a light thud on the sand, spread her arms out in front of her as if blessing the area and smiled in satisfaction that this was, indeed, the perfect spot for her morning ritual. She rolled out her tattered, little rug and sat crossed legged facing the waves. With a deep breath she inhaled the ocean's scent and closed her eyes. Ray didn't follow any particular method of meditation, she simply thanked the universe for her presence, for her surroundings, for her ability to do whatever she pleased whenever she pleased. She thanked the universe for her freedom.

That freedom had come, partly through rebelling against oppressive parental judgement, and partly because she was gifted a large sum of money when said oppressive parents died.

Communication between Ray and her family was so poor that she only found out about their deaths when a lawyer tracked her down in her forties. The news brought mixed emotions of shock, sadness and relief. She'd spent her life fighting against them.

One of the nails in the coffin of her relationship with her parents was when a sneering, smug-arsed neighbour had taken a newspaper to Ray's mother pretending to be distraught to see a grainy black and white glamour photo of Ray, topless, inside.

Ray was seeking refuge at her Aunt Minty and Uncle Spanky's Hampshire mansion at the time, having fled from the dramatic break down of marriage number one – to a rockstar, of course. Her aunt and uncle's stately home was the only place she felt welcome, with its gigantic record collection, well-stocked bar and a ballroom in which she could thrash around to Joan Jett, alone. She'd only posed for those wretched photos because her parents cut off her allowance after an argument and she was struggling to pay rent. It was not an excuse that would go down well, however. She'd dug too deep a hole that time. Aunt Minty took the outraged phone call from Ray's mother the day of the newspaper incident. Ray listened in to the shrieks and caws that came down the telephone wire and decided to return to the ballroom and turn up Joan...and pour another gin.

The inheritance windfall, which came more than two decades later, meant she could follow her carefree heart up the UK from the south of England to the north of Scotland where she instantly felt at peace.

In quiet moments on the beach, or in front of the fire at home, hints of regret and sadness crept into Ray's mind. Should she have been a kinder daughter? Should she have spared them the worry, the disappointment, the shame of never settling down in the way they would have liked? That was the major problem, however. The way they would have liked Ray to live would have been so stifling she would never have seen the world or felt the feelings of excitement or drama and wonder that had made her life what it was.

That morning on the beach, with her eyes gently closed, Ray listened to the seagulls squawking in the distance and the gentle hiss of sea foam as it licked the shore. Perfection.

A new noise rung out. A human shriek. At this time of morning?

Ray opened one eye. She opened the other eye when she spotted a round thing bobbing about on the water. It looked like a beach ball with flowers on top. Ray hadn't even lit her joint yet, so she knew this was real.

She squinted to focus her gaze. It was a head inside a swimming cap. Another shriek of joy rolled across the water to Ray's ears and two sticks jutted up around the cap. Oh! Arms. It was a woman swimming in the distance – or rather falling about in the waves and laughing.

Ray let out a chuckle. *Well, well*, she thought. *A sea goddess among us.*

She watched the floral 'ball' bobbing around for the next five minutes, a gentle smile across her lips.

Eventually, the ball became a head on shoulders and then a body with a waist and soon legs. The woman, who had the most enormous grin, waded out of the surf, breathless with thighs which had turned pink from chilliness.

"Hello," she said to Ray, in a bright and breathy voice.

"Morning," Ray beamed from her cross-legged position on her rug. "What a lovely thing to do to start your day. Do you do this often?"

The woman, who was possibly late thirties, replied: "No. This is only my second time. I shouldn't really come alone, but I saw a few dog walkers and then you, so I decided it was safe enough, with people around. I'm going to try and persuade a friend or two to start swimming with me," she said with a glint in her eye. "It gives me such a rush."

"Wonderful," Ray commented with a smile. "I love to start the day on the beach, but to start the day *inside* the ocean…just wow."

The woman replied: "You should join me some morning. I'm going to keep it up."

A flutter of excitement tickled inside Ray's chest. This was a flutter she recognised from many an adventure before. This flutter always meant she was about to do something she wouldn't regret. Something life affirming.

"No time like the present," she said rolling onto her knees to get up in a quite ungraceful manner (she was in her sixties now, give the girl a break). Once on her feet, she lifted off her loose knitted jumper, slid out of her baggy linen trousers and waded into the sea, exclaiming: "This is the life!"

She rarely wore underwear, so the woman got the comeback tour version of the grainy glamour photo which had caused her so much trouble back in her twenties.

Ray didn't look back to check her new acquaintance's expression. What people thought was never something she really considered, sometimes to her detriment. But in that very moment on that very beach, at that early hour, she felt freer than ever. The beach was empty, save for the sea goddess she'd just met, and something told her she wasn't the judgey type. A dog walker way off in the distance was of no concern. They'd have to have superhero-strength vision catch a glimpse of Ray's nude shape.

Ray pranced into the swell, arms stretched out towards the horizon as if offering mother nature a massive hug. "I'm alive!" she pronounced.

She lunged into the cool water and stretched out to swim gracefully forward. There was at least one thing her expensive schooling had taught her - well-formed swimming strokes.

Only two minutes later, and buzzing with endorphins, Ray emerged from the sea, brushed off droplets of water from her skin with her hands and quickly threw on her clothes.

"It was lovely to meet you, I'm Ray," she said to the

woman who was now huddled in a blanket sipping a steaming hot drink.

"You too. I'm Brydie."

"I'll maybe join you on a swim someday, if you really mean it," Ray said tentatively. "I live in that cottage there with the wind chimes at the doorway. If I spot you, I could pop over. I do own a swimsuit," she added with a laugh. "I promise I wouldn't make a habit of the nudey swims. I just couldn't resist getting in."

"It's a deal," said Brydie, laughing. "I can bring cake – I'm a great baker – so there's even more incentive."

"Fabulous," Ray replied, before rolling up her rug and lifting her bag onto her shoulder. "See you soon."

She strolled along the path back to her house, longing for a hot cup of oolong to warm up her tingling, ice-kissed skin. She would have a piece of cake with it. Just not the kind of cake Brydie was on about. More like the kind of cake we mentioned before that wouldn't make it through customs.

CHAPTER 3 - KIM

"**M**um! Muuu-uuum!"

Kim was in her bedroom applying rose gold, shimmering eyeshadow to her eyelids between large gulps of red wine.

"What?" She cried through the crack in the doorway.

A small head appeared. "Will you be late home?"

"Yes, Gigi, I'll be late home. Gran's here, so you'll be fine. I'm only going three doors down, to Brydie's house. It's not far."

Kim was now carefully spreading bright pink lip stain across her pursed lips. Nights out were rare these days. Being on her own with two kids meant evenings were mostly in front of the TV, but the perk of finding a friend who lived on the same street in this small seaside village meant a social life was no longer some kind of myth she'd heard about. Since becoming a mum seven years ago, tales of cocktails and dancing and actual, real live people were things of far-fetched folklore to Kim. That was until Brydie met her at a New Year Party in the village hall and the pair hit it off instantly. Dancing all night wearing plastic tiaras and chunky biker boots, they had an instant connection. As that first night wore on and conversations started drifting into territories regarding hopes and dreams – or rather a shared confusion over their personal hopes and dreams – their friendship was sealed with an invisible padlock, like those you see on bridges across Europe, declaring everlasting love. From then on, when one of them was feeling low, the other one had spare energy to charge her back up. It was precious.

Kim ran hot straighteners down sections of her shoulder-length blonde hair, watching the faint steam clouds rise and enjoying the warmth as her hot, straightened hair fell on her cool neck.

Fully ready, she went through to the living room, where seven-year-old Gigi and four-year-old Stan were bouncing about on top of their gran, excitedly, on the sofa.

"Oh mummy, you look beautiful," Stan exclaimed, in adorable, slurred, half-baked pronunciation that made Kim melt. He ran over to her and hugged her legs. "You look like the queen of....chocolate!" he finished.

"Wow," Kim remarked, bending to pick him up for a hug. "I love chocolate, so I must be really special."

She kissed his sticky cheek and put him back down.

Gigi stayed on the sofa next to her grandmother, looking slightly uncertain. "Are you going to be long?" she asked.

With a straight face, trying not to look frustrated, Kim replied: "Yes, darling. Again, you'll be in bed when I get home. That's why gran's here."

Gigi sulked.

"I'm only going to Brydie's house," Kim added. "It's on the same bloomin' street."

She walked over to lean in and kiss her daughter's cheek. Gigi clutched Kim's neck with her small, skinny arms, refusing to let go.

"Love you, Gigi. I have to go now," Kim said prising her daughters tight grip apart. Turning to her mum she said: "Thank you so much. I'll try not to be too late."

Her mum nodded. "Just have fun. We'll watch a bit of Saturday TV then I'll get them bedded. All fine. I don't want to be too late though. I've got to drive to Inverness tomorrow."

Heaving her bag full of drinks and snacks onto her shoulder, Kim paused with an awkward grin. "How late is too late?" she asked, holding her breath.

Her mum shrugged. "Maybe back by midnight?"

Kim let out a sigh of relief. "OK, great, I thought you were going to say ten and you KNOW that would never happen. We'll just be getting started at ten."

It felt good to be wearing jeans, even with the slight muffin top bulge above the waistband – caused by too many nights in front of the TV with a glass of pinot – and a new shirt with tropical leaves printed on the fabric, plus earrings with bold geometric shapes. She felt like the real 'her'.

She closed the front door, leaving family responsibility behind for a night and turned onto the street. The evening was still and quiet. A violet hue tinged the sky as the sun was contemplating turning in for the night. It washed over the grey, stone, cottages as if coating them in a thin water-colour layer. Kim smiled as she took a deep breath in and then out, enjoying the clean air entering her lungs and filling her up.

When she moved back up the 170-mile distance from the big city to Brogie, she'd been so resentful to say goodbye to cosmopolitan life and hello again to her quiet, rural past. On perfectly still spring evenings like this, however, there was something undeniably charming about the old brickwork on the former fisherman's cottages and the narrow streets that formed a crooked maze right through the village.

As a teenager, Kim was desperate to get away from this quaint, little region of Scotland where it felt like nothing ever happened. She fled to the city at eighteen and worked her way up in fashion retail while studying art. There was absolutely no part of her soul longing to move back here. She always said she felt she had a rock star soul in an ordinary girl's body. There was a persistent feeling of unfinished business within her core.

So, if life in the city was so appealing, why on earth did a girl like Kim, now in her mid-thirties, end up right back where she started? No prizes for guessing...love. An old school friend, Rick, moved to the city and bumped into her at work. There were sparks, as memories of kisses on the sand dunes in teen years came flooding back. Why are humans so tied to memories of the past that they can be so easily convinced it's something called destiny? Kim and Rick fell quickly back into infatuation with each other. Things were comfortable, almost easy, for a while. They welcomed a little daughter to the world, Gigi – short for Georgia. And then things changed.

After a couple of years, Rick began to struggle. He lost his job as a bus driver, which he denied was down to taking way too many unofficial breaks. He fell into a cycle of video games with the curtains closed, smoking weed and sometimes forgetting to pick up their toddler daughter from nursery while Kim was at work. If her mobile vibrated in her pocket at 2pm, she rolled her eyes and knew straight away he'd forgotten again.

They would argue about what appeared to be his lack of motivation to look for a job. He swore he'd been making calls that day. She never believed him.

Things got worse when he began questioning her choices. When Kim would dress up for an art show, hoping to network and make connections that could really help her start selling prints, Rick was convinced it was to attract men.

Kim tried to push all thoughts of the past to the back of her mind as she arrived at Brydie's front door. In comparison to her own place, Brydie's was so well-kept. So chic. The front door was painted sage green and adorned with a wicker and wildflowers wreath. Brydie opened the door with an air of enthusiasm, dressed in a knee-length floral tea dress, black tights and tan leather ankle boots with her curls hanging loosely around her shoulders.

"Come in, come in!" Brydie exclaimed, pulling her friend through to the kitchen where two glasses of bubbly were ready and waiting on the breakfast bar.

The pair settled into their usual positions - Brydie on the left stool, Kim on the right, both facing the kitchen window that looked onto the sea.

Talk had already turned to relationships...as it always seemed to.

"I should have seen the signs way back then," Kim said to Brydie as she sipped her first prosecco of the night.

She continued: "If I hadn't fallen pregnant with Stan I would never have moved back up here. That's when he persuaded me we needed our families around us. To be fair, he had a point. I wouldn't function if I lived further away from mum. She's my hero." Kim took another sip then sighed. "Obviously, it was the worst decision for our relationship. He just stopped trying. When he started working for his dad and growing a beer gut and grumping at me constantly, I thought, what has my life become? I'm still young and this is not what was supposed to happen."

Brydie held up her glass. "Cheers to you and the road ahead," she said. "You're awesome, you're talented, you have so much still to do."

Kim smiled. Brydie never complained about having to listen to these therapy-esque pourings of her feelings.

"Right, enough of that crap," Kim exclaimed. "No more looking back. We've got a few hours with which to laugh and boogie. Not wasting any more of it on 'Prick'."

Brydie turned up the stereo which was now blasting out hits from the '90s and 2000s – allowing the women to relive their teenage joy...and angst - and hit the light switch, plunging her rustic cottage kitchen into darkness. She grabbed a small remote control and zapped on some multicoloured disco lights which were wired under the top cabinets, casting explosions of neon colours across the room. They began hopping and stomping around the small room, letting all their frustrations disappear.

Several songs later, they took a break and sat at the breakfast bar which jutted out like a pontoon into the middle of the room. Brydie began pouring different spirits and fruit juices into a glass jug. She had an excited grin on her face while she was chopping juicy lime wedges.

"I did something crazy the other day," she said, looking up to catch Kim's eye. "I stripped off on the beach and went for a swim."

Kim's mouth fell open. "What? Naked?"

"No," Brydie was shaking her head with a laugh. "I kept my undies on. Something was just drawing me to the water. I just HAD to get in."

"Wasn't it flamin' freezing?" Kim asked with a sneer.

"Yes. It was bloody Baltic," Brydie replied, her face creasing up with amusement. "But it was fantastic. I just felt so bright. My skin was tingling and I felt sort of scared but free at the same time. I went back in again today. In fact, I met this really cool woman as I got out, a sort of floaty hippy. She stripped off naked, I kid you not, and went in for a swim after I got out."

Kim snorted and struggled to swallow a sip of her drink. "Completely starkers?"

Brydie nodded with a chuckle. "She was really lovely. She had this calming energy about her. Anyway, I said to her I'm going to try and do it regularly and she said she might join me...but she'll cover her bits next time."

Brydie plopped a thick lime wedge into a glass before flooding it with orangey-red liquid and handing it to Kim. "Here, taste this."

Kim sat thoughtfully for a moment. "So, would you go proper swimming?"

Brydie laughed. "What do you mean?"

"I mean like this." Kim mimicked a swimmer doing fast front crawl.

"No, no," Brydie said, shaking her head decidedly. "I'm not a strong swimmer. I'd just like to take a dip and do casual breaststroke every so often."

Kim laughed. "Not a strong swimmer! Why the hell would you run into the sea then? You're mad."

Brydie shrugged. "It was exactly what I needed at that moment. You should try it."

"Hmmm. We'll see," said Kim unsurely, as she took a sip of her cocktail and her face creased up. "It's strong," she gasped in a raspy whisper. "My throat is burning."

Brydie laughed and gave Kim an overenthusiastic thumbs up before turning the music louder – this time, a bit of seventies disco – and shuffling back over to the prime dancing spot by the kitchen sink. Kim leapt out of her seat to join her soul sister in the boogying.

CHAPTER 4 – WADING IN

I t was the morning after the kitchen disco. Brydie rolled over in her crumpled, sweaty bed sheets. Doug was still deep in the land of slumber, vibrations of snoring throbbing around the room.

Brydie's tongue felt like sandpaper. Why had they opened that third bottle of prosecco? After the cocktails, too.

She checked the time. 6.30am. Brydie rolled out of bed, pain stabbing at her eyes as she fought to fully open them. Paracetamol and a cup of tea were screaming out to her.

Once settled on the slouchy sofa in the living room with her rescue remedy of steaming hot tea and pills, Brydie looked out the window at the sunny morning. It was full of promise. *It's always such a juxtaposition on a hangover*, Brydie thought, w*hen the sun is shining but you feel like shit.*

She vowed in that moment to force herself to walk on the beach later on. She would persuade Doug to join her. The promise of a flask of coffee and cakes would do the trick.

A few hours, and a hot, cooked breakfast later, Doug and Brydie were in their stride, churning up the distance on the flat stretch of sand which curved round like a rainbow from their village to the more popular destination of Findhoun.

The couple exchanged chat of their week ahead and stories of last night. Doug had been dragged into the kitchen to perform Material Girl, much to his dismay, and had he not consumed three beers watching a Bond movie he would have refused. Being the good sport that he is, he embraced his inner Madonna and lived up to his wife's expectations by prancing around the kitchen with a wooden spoon microphone.

"Just don't put that online," he said with a grimace as they padded along the firm sand the morning after.

Brydie's eyes widened. "Too late," she said, attempting to stifle a giggle. "Kim already posted it."

Doug laughed and planted his palm over his face. He clearly wasn't *too* worried.

They stopped at the concrete blocks which were left on the beach as a brutal legacy from World War II. The beach was littered with concrete which had been used to protect the area from invasion all those years ago, and now the wonky blocks were used for picnickers to sit on. Pouring hot coffee into a metal camp mug, Brydie examined the sea, which was green in colour today, churning up with white frothy frills. It was calling her. She was desperate to get back in. Something had released in her that day in the cool water.

"You coming in for a swim?" she jested.

"No chance," said Doug. "Do you want my goolies to function properly or do you want them to die off in the cold?"

Brydie feigned an expression of consideration at the thought, before laughing and replying: "You can keep your balls. For now."

A secret disappointment tugged at her internally. She would have to come back on her own during the week. She needed that silky fix of ocean therapy, but no-one seemed to understand. Perhaps she'd get in touch with her new nude friend with the windchime house. She was longing to leap back in.

Meanwhile, Kim, feeling equally as rough, was packing up the kids' bags for two days at their dad's.

Two honks of the car horn rang outside. That was the signal that it was handover time. Neither were ready to make small talk at this point, so Rick stayed in the car and Kim stayed at the front door, keeping a safe distance between their hurting souls. Feelings were still too raw – Kim's bitter resentment and Rick's outrage that he, apparently, was not enough for her.

"Come on guys, get your bags, time to go," Kim said, making every effort to maintain a steady calmness in her voice. Inside she was spinning. She was looking forward to a break from being on duty, but at the same time, what would the kids be doing without her? What would Rick be saying? Would he try to poison them against her? Was he fun? Was he loving? Or was he still dark and silent?

She squeezed their tiny, warm bodies and fixed their backpacks properly on their small shoulders before watching them run down the path to his rusty Ford Focus.

She couldn't watch them drive off. Instead, Kim stood with her back against the closed front door with her eyes closed, breathing deep for half a minute. When she opened them, the harsh reality of the need for tidying and cleaning made her groan.

Instead, she slumped on the sofa and picked up her phone, laughing at the memory of Doug slamming his leg up on the kitchen counter and smashing a jug for the finale of his Madonna track. She watched the video, giggling softly.

"Fancy a walk?" she texted Brydie.

Her phone pinged only seconds later. "Already been on

one. Fancy a swim???" The message ended with several laughing emojis.

Kim's heart raced. Maybe she should. Why the hell not? Cleaning could wait. She needed an assault on her mind. Something to distract her from the self-deprecating hate that would sink in at any moment. The guilt she felt for dragging her kids down a split family road always haunted her within moments of their departure.

"Go on then," she replied.

One hour later, standing at the edge of the tide, holding hands and laughing nervously, Brydie and Kim shivered in their swimsuits.

"Trust me," Brydie said. "You will *love* this."

Tentatively, they edged into the water.

Yelps of pain spiked the cool breeze as the water circled round their shins, licking upwards like flames of ice.

Brydie pulled Kim's arm and began to run into the waves, dragging her friend along for the ride. In only a matter of minutes, the pair were shrieking with laughter as frothy, white water slammed into their thighs, wiping away any worries or negative thoughts that may have been lurking.

Kim jumped high to avoid being completely engulfed by an unexpectedly intimidating wave. She couldn't remember the last time she jumped. Why was it that we jump, run and dance as kids, but as adults these actions are rare? She brushed the crusty, salty strands of hair from her face and dove into the aqua which was now calm in the aftermath of the wave, plunging her shoulders and arms into the cool water. It felt amazing. Her skin buzzed with what felt like electricity. The friends smiled at each other through laughs as salty water lapped around their shoulders. Kim felt the familiar hot pricking of tears threaten her eyes. All the guilt, all the worry came to the surface. Was she a selfish mum? Could she have ridden it out in a shitty relationship for their sake? She looked out at the line of the horizon where the sea met the sky and, suddenly, she felt insignificant. It was as if being so small in such a large body of water made the weight of her worries drift away. She allowed the tears to break their banks and roll down her eyelids. Salty tears mingled with salty sea-spray in hot tracks running down her cheeks. The ocean gave her permission to release all this angst.

Brydie was so busy jumping high waves, she didn't notice this outpouring of emotion from her dear friend, but this was perfect for Kim. She didn't need to talk. She didn't want to explain herself. It was cleansing. The sea was literally washing her pain, her tears, away.

As great, rumbling growls of rising waves tumbled past the women then gave way to gentle hissing sounds of bubbling foam settling onto calm water, Kim's emotions softened. She could feel herself letting go with each wave.

Suddenly, an enormous one, two feet taller than the two women, engulfed them both and knocked them off their feet. They emerged, breathless and laughing hysterically. They grabbed for each other in unison, finding support in each other's arms as the laughter poured from their beings.

Kim felt lighter in every way. She felt changed.

As the friends sat in warm jumpers and blankets on the shore, cradling metal mugs of hot tea in their hands, they didn't need to say a thing. Smiles decorated their relaxed faces delicately as they stared out at the rolling waves.

There's nothing like a wave wipeout to reset the mind, Kim thought as she fought the stinging of tears once more, but this time of relief and gratitude.

CHAPTER 5 –
TAKING SHAPE

"**S**hall I click 'buy'?" Brydie asked tentatively as she sat at Kim's kitchen table, still feeling the tingling effects of the chilly sea on her skin – two hours after their morning dip.

Kim's kitchen was awash with spring sunlight pouring in the window above the sink. It shone a spotlight on the scribbled children's drawings which were pinned to the fridge door with novelty magnets in the shapes of animals and beef burgers. The sunlight also danced on the dishes which lay upside down in a chaotic and unstable formation, drying, on the draining board and the washing machine whirred busily.

Kim's face creased in uncertainty.

"It's so much money," she said, rubbing her tingling fingers, thinking of the school uniform money she needed to start putting aside for summer.

Brydie laid out her hand on the table in Kim's direction, as if to lay down the law. "I told you, I'll buy these - on Doug's card," she added with a chuckle, "and you can pay me back in instalments whenever you can. Apparently surf gloves and boots will make the world of difference. I still can't feel my bloody toes."

Kim nodded. "Yeah, my fingers felt like they had dropped off into the sea – couldn't feel any sensation in them for ages."

"So, let's do it," Brydie said with confidence. "Done.

Ordered. Two pairs of surf boots and two pairs of surf gloves. Next up…dry robes…but they cost an absolute fortune, we'd have to sell one of your kids."

Kim let out a snort of laughter. "Do we really need robes?"

"Yes. Absolutely," Brydie insisted. "I've been reading up on all this and it's the only way we're going to be able to keep going when it gets colder."

"Colder?" Kim said with a shudder.

"All the groups online swear by these fleecy robes to stop you getting so cold when you get out. And they're massive so you can get changed inside them without accidentally flashing your boobies. We can wait a few months for those though. I'll hide the spending by doing it gradually." Brydie winked at Kim with an air of mischief.

The pair vowed to keep this new hobby of theirs going.

"I feel like I'm given an electric shock of life energy whenever I'm in that water," Brydie said, oozing with enthusiasm.

"I know what you mean," Kim agreed. "And anything I'm worrying about seems to just disappear. I feel like I leave my earth body behind and become some sort of sea creature. Do you know what I mean? Is that too much?"

Brydie shook her head. "I do know what you mean."

Kim's eyes widened, and, holding her index finger aloft, she pondered her thoughts for a few moments before saying: "Maybe we should start a group, like the ones you've seen online. Put it on the Brogie Bay socials and see if any other people fancy it. Could be fun."

Brydie pointed at Kim decisively. "You are right, my friend. That's an awesome idea. What will we call ourselves? Mermaids? Too boring."

The two women sat in contemplative silence for a moment.

"Brogie…seals….?" Kim offered.

"Brogie Beach Babes?" Brydie bounced back, before frowning. "Nah, that's too Baywatch."

"Brogie Bay Dookers? The Dookers for short?" suggested Kim with a shrug.

"Yeah, that'll do," Brydie said, nodding thoughtfully. "I'll get on the case and start a page. Nice one."

Their thoughtful mood was interrupted by the shrill ring of Kim's doorbell.

Her stomach lurched. "That'll be Rick with the kids. Handover time."

She left the sunny kitchen and padded softly through the hall, conflicted by one part joy at the thought of seeing her kids, and the other part dread at the awkward interaction with her ex that lay behind that wooden door.

She opened it, keeping her eyes at a low child-eye level, grinning at her two little people who simply dumped their backpacks at the door and burst over the threshold shouting about toys they were longing to reunite with as they ran off to their shared room.

"Hi," Rick said tentatively.

"Hi, thanks for bringing them." Kim replied, one hand on the door handle ready to gently push it shut.

"How are you?" he asked, startling Kim. They hadn't made small talk at handover time before.

"Fine, yeah. You?"

"I've been better," he replied. "I miss you."

Kim felt her throat tighten and her mouth dry up. Not this again. She looked into his eyes, feeling her forehead crease into a stiff frown. She had no words. A light sigh left her dry lips.

"Listen," he continued. "I'd love to come in and just talk to you. No pressure. Just a chat. A coffee?"

"I've got a friend over," Kim replied, crossing her arms defensively.

Rick stiffened. A change came over his face. He tilted his head back slightly, thrusting his wiry, black beard outward.

"A female friend," Kim added quickly, realising what storm of jealous thoughts must have been starting to stir in his mind. Not that it was any of his business anymore.

He softened. "Another time? I feel like we barely discussed things. I don't know if there is anything else I could have done to save us?"

Really? Kim thought? *Really?*

"Look," she said, forcing herself to relive this agony in a calm, reasonable way. "I really don't think there's anything else to say. We didn't work anymore. We barely spent time together, and when we did it was miserable. You have….things to work on. So do I. I want to just get back to being me. I want to be lighter again."

Her words hung awkwardly in the space between them.

"You're a great dad," she added, not even sure if that was true. "And you'll be fine."

He shrugged and said curtly: "See you next time," then marched down the garden path to his car without looking back.

Kim let out a long breath she hadn't realised she was withholding. The sound of her kids arguing snapped her out of the fog of sorrow she always felt after having to sprinkle more words of hurt over her teenage love. No matter how much she knew it wasn't right between them, it still hurt to have to distance from him.

She slammed the front door shut and aimed her mother-wrath voice down the hallway: "If I have to come in there and separate you two I will *not* be happy!"

She jumped to see Brydie appear from around the corner in the hall. The pair laughed.

"That's my strict voice," Kim admitted with a grimace.

"It's good," Brydie said, almost mockingly. "I'll be on my best behaviour so you don't need to pull out the big guns on *me*. Anyway, I have to go now. Catch you later in the week for another swim."

"Fab," Kim replied, reaching out to hug her friend. The warmth of another adult body who was on her side felt so good. It reminded her she wasn't a bad person. If Brydie could like her this much and hug her and spend time with her, then surely she wasn't the piece of shit she felt she was after that encounter with her ex. She held the hug a little too long.

"You alright?" Brydie asked, pulling herself away to check her friend's facial expression.

"Yeah, I'm good," Kim replied with a gentle smile. And in that moment, she really was.

CHAPTER 6 - MARTHA

As Martha pushed the cumbersome trolley full of cleaning equipment into the Domestic Services Room, she let out a laboured sigh. She'd been on a double shift since 7am with only half an hour between the shifts. First, she'd cleaned ward five top to bottom, manoeuvring heavy beds and bed-side units to mop underneath and empty goodness knows how many bins. Thankfully there had been no curtain changes today. That was an ordeal in itself. There was a long-term patient in room three who regularly sprayed shit everywhere – goodness knows how – and that meant a full curtain change, which involved travelling down three flights of stairs for a fresh pair and standing on a stepladder to reach the top of the rail. Her arm muscles always burned like hell during that chore.

Martha took on this hospital domestic job when she turned forty-five, after her kids had flown the nest. The decent hourly rate was the main reason she'd stayed thirteen years so far. As the years were slipping by, the physical nature of the job was causing aches and pains in surprising places. A new ache popped up every other month, as if her body was mocking her. "Surprise! I bet you didn't know your arse cheek could hurt so much!"

In this rural location, if a job paid well and you were surrounded by good people, it was golden. Martha loved her team of women. They were the most caring people she'd met. There were bitching sessions between the younger, more competitive domestics, but Martha and her workmates were able to sweep those issues aside with an eye roll and a sigh.

Martha locked the DSR and made her way to the underground changing room - down two flights of stairs, just along the corridor from the mortuary. Occasionally, she would be saying a cheery hello to Dave, one of the porters, in this corridor then realise the long, zipped up bag on the metal bed he'd been transporting was clearly someone's tragic journey to the resting place on the bottom floor. It never failed to give her a chill.

"What are you up to tonight Martha?" Carole asked.

"I'm cooking mince and tatties then catching up on episodes of my drama," she replied with a sigh. "You?"

"I'm doing pork chops," Carole replied, "and then I'll probably carry on with the blanket I'm making."

A stab of guilt pierced Martha's thoughts. She had a wardrobe full of half-finished knitting projects. She'd learned as a child to knit any stitch you could name. She rarely even followed patterns anymore, she knew how to create garments by instinct. For the past few months, however, something was stopping her. It was as if she couldn't physically pick up the needles. Once a week she would open the wardrobe door, stare at the brightly coloured wool which had been cast onto several needles and then dumped in a pile. This pile had so much potential. There was a teal hat with only two rows completed, a fuchsia scarf which was supposed to be for her daughter's birthday, but that date had been and gone, and there was a mustard pair of gloves with only a wrist band so far. Martha's heart just wasn't in it.

Ron, her husband of thirty-three years, had asked her one day what was happening. He'd never known her to be so disinterested in making things.

36

"It'll come back to me," she insisted with a forced smile. "I'm just tired. When I've got those two weeks off in the summer, I'm sure I'll finish all those bits and bobs."

After dinner that night, during her favourite crime drama, Martha's mind wandered away from the interrogation scene and into her own reality.

I should really finish those gloves. Or have I lost that skill? Am I done for? All work, no play, no crafting. Is this it? Oh shut up Martha, you're bloody lucky. Ron's healthy, you're healthy, the kids are doing fine, there's a grandkid on the way. Quit your complaining.

The camera zoomed slowly in as the TV detective looked intensely off to the side with a furrowed brow and the credits rolled over the top of the scene. *Oh bugger, I missed that. What did they find out?* Martha fumbled frantically for the remote. She twisted her body to the left to grab for it and pulled something in her shoulder. *For Pete's sake*, she thought as a sharp pain soared through her nerves. *This body of mine.*

The next morning, Martha sipped hot, milky tea, sitting peacefully on her huge, slouchy beige sofa in front of the TV. It was her day off from the hospital. Her chance to watch some daytime programmes. Her back ached. She shifted her bottom, attempting to ease the tight spasms that nudged at her continually.

The episode she was watching about a wealthy couple looking for their dream home with an unrealistically long list of 'must-haves' wasn't doing it for her. "Pair of greedy so-and-sos," she muttered to herself as the woman on screen said: "No, this house is ghastly. We need an extra room for crafting and the kitchen needs to have an island."

"Come and have a look at my house, you greedy mare,"

Martha continued towards the screen. "The crafting room is a shoe box over there, and a kitchen island? A kitchen island? The only island you'll find here is my ass when I'm in the bath."

She started to chuckle at the release, shaking her head and sighing with pleasure.

She switched off the TV and picked up her phone to begin her regular ritual of scrolling social media to see what her grown-up kids were up to. It was the only way she really found out. There was nothing new to see since she last checked a few hours ago. Some friends had posted about bake sales at the weekend, which piqued her interest slightly. Then Martha looked down at her tight sweatshirt, grimaced and scrolled on from the bake sale post. Cake was not the answer. Not when she'd been complaining to Ron constantly of wanting to lose a stone before their next wedding anniversary…which was creeping ever closer.

The Brogie News page would possibly have some interesting gossip, she decided, and searched for it. There was always some car vandalism or lost cat, or an opportunity to be nosey and see into people's homes if they posted pictures of items they were selling. She'd discovered that Amanda down the street had a hideous 1980s-style living room of pastel yellow, pink and grey that really amused her, so maybe today there would be something suitably enlightening.

After a few uninteresting posts about pub quizzes something appeared that made Martha sit up a little straighter, despite the twinge in her back.

"Brogie Bay Dookers want you to join them for a splash in the sea," she read in a quiet, breathy voice. "Casual fun for like-minded people who want to experience cold water swimming. Mental health benefits, pain benefits, a chance to make friends. We're heading down to the slappy (the slipway by the harbour) at 10am on Wednesday if you can make it. No equipment really needed, although surf boots and gloves are recommended for warmth."

Martha had seen something on TV previously explaining the benefits of cold water therapy on pain. She pursed her lips in wonder. Could she do this?

She owned a swimsuit from her holiday with Ron five years ago, but did it still fit, was the question.

Martha moved through to the bedroom and rummaged around in her bottom drawer where the garments she rarely needed, but couldn't part with, lived.

Her black and red floral swimsuit appeared beneath summer blouses which hadn't seen the light of day for a few years. She'd put on a few pounds lately. The pain in her back had taken away any motivation to get out and about on walks on her days off. Her job at the hospital was physical enough, she justified to herself.

Martha pulled off her jogging bottoms and sweatshirt and clumsily tumbled into the swimsuit. Standing in front of the bedroom mirror, she let out a groan to see a spare tyre bulge around her middle. That hadn't been there the last time she wore this suit. She twisted her waist – as much as the twinges would allow her – to check her bottom and ensure there was enough fabric coverage. "Crikey," she exclaimed, grimacing to see the dimples and folds in her ample cheeks.

A surge of shame seemed to tighten like a fist around her stomach as memories of being in a swimsuit at the local public swimming pool as a ten-year-old girl played in her mind, taunting her. It was something that stayed with her right through teens and adulthood. She had been so happy that day, in a brand new blue swimsuit. Her granny was waving proudly from the spectator area - women in her family never got in the pool it seemed, citing body shame as the reason. Martha remembers waving back at her granny with a beaming smile before a boy ran past her shouting: "Fat, lazy slob. You're going to sink to the bottom!" Martha suddenly felt pure sorrow for that ten-year-old girl who'd had her pride stolen from her in that moment. The entire day out was dampened by that hurtful comment. Instead of wanting to splash around with abandon, young Martha walked along the edge of the pool self-consciously, sure that everyone else must think the same thing: fat, lazy slob.

In the forty-eight years since then, swimming costumes had always felt so exposing, so wrong. She'd often moaned to Ron: "why can't all swimsuits have full arms and legs? Why do we have to be practically naked?"

Martha stood straighter, as if an invisible boot camp leader had ordered her to attention.

"Right. I'm doing this! I'm going for the swim," she exclaimed to the bedroom. "I'm going to take my life back. I'm fed up of feeling fat and bored. I'm not dead yet!"

Ron popped his head around the bedroom door, saying cheerily: "What's that my love?"

Martha shrieked. "Ron! What are you doing home? Oh my god, don't look at me."

Ron laughed. "It's lunchtime. I'm home for my soup. Why are you wearing that?"

Martha buried her face in her hands with embarrassment.

Ron entered the room and walked over to his wife with a cheeky grin on his face. "Ooh er. It's nice to see my woman's bare legs," he said, putting his hands around her waist.

"Ron," she said with a pained laugh.

"Seriously, you look great," he said. "My curvy woman."

She laughed and rolled her eyes. Ron pushed a strand of Martha's chin-length chestnut hair behind her ear and looked her in the eyes. "You're still as beautiful as ever to me."

Martha was always uncomfortable with compliments. "I feel silly."

"Don't," Ron insisted. He looked down at the floral suit. "But I have to ask...why the dookers?"

"Well...." Martha replied, rolling her eyes... "I saw this post on the Brogie page online about people getting together for a dook. I thought it might help with my aches. And I need something new. I'm fed up of myself."

Ron's eyebrows raised. "Wow. Do it. Go for it. It'll be bloomin' freezin' but you're a hardy lass. You used to always like a swim on holiday. Might not be as pleasant as in Tenerife, but you only live once."

He planted a kiss on Martha's cheek and left her in the bedroom, looking at her reflection in the full-length mirror. Martha shook her head in disapproval at her wobbly bits.

Decisively, Martha pulled off the swimsuit, folded it, found her sports holdall at the bottom of the wardrobe and put the suit in there, along with a towel from the hall cupboard. The swim was only a few days away. She wouldn't have too much time to allow doubts to gnaw away at her and put her off. The sooner the better. Strike while the iron is hot...or while the waves are ice cold in this case.

CHAPTER 7 - MIKE

In his distinctive red uniform with tinny, shrill notes of music escaping his earphones, Mike bobbed his head gently to the beat of a 1980s rock classic and pushed his postal cart up the seafront street of former fishermen's cottages. This was his favourite part of the delivery route. To his left were the quaint cottages, full of his favourite people to bring post to – for wildly differing reasons – and to his right was the open expanse of water that was sheltered by the harbour and the headland, making it a tranquil stretch of beach, popular with paddle boarders and kayakers. Mike squinted to check the bay and nodded in respect to see one such paddle boarder sitting down on their board, legs dangling in the water at either side, the paddle resting on their lap as they looked out into the horizon. This fine morning, the clouds reflected off the calm water, giving it a silvery, grey tone. He often wished he could be brave enough to invest in a board and give it a go, but something always held him back.

Mike had called this village home for ten years, having retired from the air force where he was stationed near Brogie Bay. The base had brought him up from his birthplace in the English midlands, and as soon as he familiarised himself with the miles upon miles of golden sand that edged this stunning part of north-east Scotland, he knew he would never leave. There was also the deeper reason of heartache that made him want to stay hundreds of miles up north. With three grown-up children down south who barely spoke to him and an ex-wife who loathed him, there was nothing to pull him back there. He had a nice life here. A small flat in a converted fish warehouse, with a little balcony overlooking the sea, a steady supply of beers, the occasional rolled-up cigarette, a guitar and his thoughts. Though sometimes those thoughts were more poisonous than anything else. Questions gnawed away at him. What could he have done better? How could he repair the relationships with his kids? When they were young he was often away on tours of military duty or posted around the country. He sent birthday and Christmas presents and attempted to phone the kids, but phone calls were met with reluctance, especially as they grew into their teen years. Their mother's new partners – of which there were quite a few over the years – always took favour for "always being there, unlike you, Mike," and splashing the cash "unlike you, Mike". Not feeling he could compete, he shied away. Resigned from duty. He regretted that now, even though he still couldn't see how he would have done things differently. More often than not, Mike preferred to live in a safe bubble of music, food and movies. That was enough for him.

He also treated himself over the past three years to a full sleeve of tattoos on his left arm, depicting his life in music - logos of ACDC, Metallica, guitars, skulls. This was his own form of quiet rebellion in an otherwise peaceful existence. His warm smile and head of floppy salt and pepper-coloured hair offset the hard tattoo image, creating a balance which he felt made him approachable but edgy enough to satisfy his ageing rocker soul.

Mike approached Rose Cottage, where Brenda would welcome him with an offer of a cup of tea, which he respectfully turned down ninety percent of the time, but enjoyed that the offer never ceased. He paused the music, knowing small talk was on its way. As predicted, Brenda appeared at her front door, hunched over slightly in her lilac cardigan and patting her perfectly coiffed mound of fluffy white hair. The door was painted a beautiful forget-me-not blue and framed by an archway of willow. Gentle and lovely, just like Brenda.

"How are you today Mike?" she asked, flashing a warm smile.

Mike grinned, "I'm not bad. How could I complain when I've got this to look at?" He spread his arm out towards the bay. "It's a gorgeous day."

"Oh my, look at that person out on their little boat thing," Brenda said, putting her hand above her eyes and squinting as if that would zoom in and give her a better view.

"It's a paddle board Brenda," Mike said, following her gaze. "Alright for some," he added, feeling the need to drop a bit of light chit chat in there to round off the conversation.

He sifted through the mail and handed Brenda a bundle of letters. She beamed as if he'd given her a bottle of Channel wrapped in luxurious paper with a golden bow.

"You have a nice day then," he said as he pushed onwards.

Next up was Ray's... interesting cottage. In comparison to Brenda's neatly painted and framed doorway, Ray's had peeling, faded red paint and plant pots either side of the door which were home to an abundance of weeds which had long since taken over the original shrubs that were meant to take pride of residence in them.

Who knew what state she'd be in today. Some days she was groggy and muted, or didn't come to the door at all. Others, she was like a beautiful, mystical creature floating around, her long, wavy, dyed red hair trailing after her like a ghost train on fire.

No sign of life yet. Mike was actually relieved. There was something about Ray that reduced him to a nervous wreck, like a young boy infatuated by his school teacher. Even though they were a similar age, as far as Mike could tell, she had a domineering presence that sucked the power out of him.

He found her two pieces of mail for the day and moved to post them through the rusty letterbox, but his action caused the door to swing open.

"Hello?" he called into the hallway, suddenly inhaling a plume of what definitely smelled like weed fumes. He stifled a laugh. This did not surprise him at all.

Ray drifted down the hallway with purpose, her long, midnight blue, satin dressing gown swishing behind her and leaving the sight of her black satin night dress for Mike's eyes to dart nervously over, before he deliberately began to focus on the mosaic mirror straight ahead on the wall instead.

"Hi Sweetie," she oozed. "What have you brought for me today? No bills I hope. I won't be a very happy bunny if it's bills."

Mike gulped. He braved some eye contact with Ray as he handed her the letters. The ever so slight lines around her sparkling hazel eyes and the subtle creases in her neck gave her a gentle beauty that told of experience and maturity.

"You know," he said, pausing to tap the door, "you really shouldn't leave your front door open. Anyone could come in. Or animals or such."

Ray sighed and placed a hand on her forehead in slight distress. "I think it's broken. I keep thinking I've closed it, then I come back to find it like this." She shrugged helplessly, gesturing to the wide open door.

Mike pushed it back and forth examining the lock and handle. "I could come back later with my toolbox and see if I can figure it out...if you like," he found himself spilling forth before he could check the meaning of what he was actually saying.

"Would you?" Ray said, clutching her chest joyfully. "That would be wonderful. I could brew us up some dandelion tea and I've got a nice turmeric loaf too. I'll make it worth your while."

Mike's mouth was suddenly dry. He let out a nervous laugh. "OK. I'll pop round after my shift. Any time in particular suit you?"

"Darling," Ray said with a whimsical eye roll, "I'll be here all day. There's nowhere to bloody *go* in this village, apart from the beach. And I've already done that. I was there with the sunrise."

He glanced at her nightie curiously and almost queried why she was in nightwear if she'd been out already but thought better of it. Shaking the thought subtly from his head, he smiled, unable to make eye contact, and agreed to pop by later and moved on towards the next stone cottage.

He chastised himself inwardly for falling into her trap. *Women*, he thought. *They come over all nice, but in the end all you become to them is a toolbox and a wallet. Don't get sucked in. Be nice, because, well, she's a nice woman – a very nice woman – but... be smart. Keep your head on dude.*

CHAPTER 8 – LISA

All Lisa could hear was the gentle tinkling noise of the water lapping at the edges of her board. She had paddled all the way out to the centre of the bay, far from the pale yellow strip of sand in the distance, but close enough to the domineering harbour wall to her right, which was a blessing as it was protecting her from the thundering white horses of waves that crashed against it at the other side. This particular spot Lisa was 'parked' in, was smooth, calm, stunning. She could see all the way along the curved coast to Rossy-isle beach, with its lush fringe of pine trees towering above it, and Findhoun beach, which formed a peninsula and the rest of the world seemed to drop away behind it.

She was quite new to paddle boarding, but she'd been on a course and learned enough safety tips to feel confident coming out alone. She tugged on the strap of her inflatable life vest, tightening it slightly for comfort and took a long, satisfying breath of cool, salty air.

Not being solid enough on her feet yet to stand on the board for long periods of time, Lisa was kneeling, using the paddle to push her through the silky water effortlessly. She knew, however, that if one direction is easy, chances are the way back will be difficult. The tide was going out, which was why it took her no effort at all to get to this spot. She knew her arm muscles would feel the burn on the way back, against the tide. It really didn't matter. It was worth it.

She pulled her paddle up and lay it out on the board, while she carefully manoeuvred into a sitting position. She'd done this many times before and seventy percent of times had resulted in her toppling into the depths.

As her bottom landed slowly into a sitting position she smiled proudly and dangled her feet either side of the board. Her wetsuit and boots protected her skin from the shock of coldness. In fact, that was one thing she didn't like about wearing a wetsuit. She couldn't feel the sea. She was just a human, wrapped in human attire, visiting the ocean. So often, she'd been tempted to come out on the board in just a pair of shorts, with the idea of embracing the water. But, with it being only the start of spring, she knew it would be silly. Being out on the board was a commitment. She wasn't just in the sea for ten minutes, she could be out here for a long time. And if she ran into trouble it would be far better to have warm protection than suffer from the cold quickly, she told herself.

Lisa lay the paddle across her thighs, clutching it like a pram handle. The muscle memory of that action made her think of Clara, her fifteen-year-old daughter from her first marriage. Clara was going through a rough patch since they had moved up to Brogie from Glasgow with Lisa's new wife Heather.

Clara actually seemed to prefer Heather to her mum at the moment. Everything Lisa did these days seemed to rile Clara up the wrong way. The three women – two in their forties and one emerging into young adulthood – had given up city life for a rural seaside existence. Lisa wondered if that was the crux of the problem. Perhaps Clara resented her mother for snatching her away from cinemas, shops, concerts, friends and instead forced her to live in a village with one shop and a twenty-minute bus journey to the nearest secondary school.

Lisa exhaled deeply, then pushed the breath back out slowly. Her long, sandy-coloured hair was tucked up inside a purple bobble hat for cosiness as she sat on her gently rocking board. She closed her eyes and listened to the seagulls crying softly in the distance and the soft percussion of the water hitting her board. She smiled. It reminded her of playing the triangle at school. Tiny, jangling notes. Then deeper, hollow notes, like a large wooden glockenspiel.

School. Why did she have to go and think of school? It plucked her right out of her calm moment. She would need to get back home soon to start writing lesson plans. She taught eight-year-olds, if you could call breaking up fights and counselling crying kids teaching. She had a really difficult class this year – her first year of teaching in this area. She'd worked in inner-city schools for years and had expected it to be super easy settling into a rural school. The only job she'd managed to secure in the great move up north had been in the least affluent part of a large town nearby. She was covering a maternity leave and was therefore trying to establish her authority and calm the children into her ways. She felt her chest tighten at the thought of school, then shook her head and took some more deep breaths to bring herself back to this moment.

She opened her eyes and felt the sunlight prick at them like needles. They must have been closed for quite some time, she realised. She gasped to see a fin disappearing into the glossy depths just about ten feet in front of the nose of her board. Her heart quickened.

Lisa listened and watched. Nothing. About twenty seconds later a nose then head and fin split through the water to her left, causing a swishing noise as the water was pushed all around.

She shrieked and threw her hand over her mouth in disbelief. "Hello gorgeous," she whispered to the dolphin. "This is insane."

The dolphin disappeared below the surface again, whipping the top layer of water with its tail, causing her board to rock gently from side to side. She laughed, breathlessly and turned her head as far as she could towards the back of the board. She waited, still holding her breath. Another thirty seconds went by, Lisa sat poised, tense, with a beaming smile the whole time. She saw a dark shape to her right now, moving quickly back out towards the front of her board. Another dolphin leapt out of the water up ahead, about thirty feet away, causing her to gasp. Two dolphins! The dark smear emerged again, all shiny nose and fin and Lisa saw its dark, beady eye – a mesmerising moment. Its body made a glorious smooth curve action and disappeared again, heading out towards its partner. Lisa watched as the pair leapt gracefully all the way back out to the horizon until she could no longer make out any fins.

All her anxieties about whether it had been the right move to bring the family up north were dealt with in those gentle leaps. Of course this was the right place to be. The sea was healing her grieving soul. Nowhere else on earth ever seemed to extract the negative feelings quite like this. Her brain hummed with positive energy. She felt uplifted, invincible – like she could cope with anything as long as she could return to the bay and do this all over again.

She eyed the bay, which brought her back to the present moment. There was a lot more sand visible that when she'd first paddled out here, meaning the tide was well on its way out. The sensible thing to do would be to paddle back in now before she drifted any further with the outgoing tide.

She braced herself, got back up onto her knees – without toppling into the water – and put in the effort to soar back to land.

Then came the rigmarole of deflating the board, rolling it up, peeling her limbs out of the wetsuit, getting changed and packing it all away. It was such an ordeal, however, still riding high on the joy of her dolphin encounter, she breezed through it all with a glazed smile.

Before heading home, she decided to pop into the shop for a bottle of wine for that evening's meal. It would help her with her lesson planning. Plus, Heather was cooking a roast that night. *It would be a crime not to bring home a bottle*, she thought with a smirk.

In the booze aisle of the miniscule version of a supermarket, which had a grand total of two aisles and customers had to breath in and hug the shelves to let each other past, she overheard two older women's conversation.

"Have you seen that the old hotel up on the hill has folk moved in now?" one asked.

"Oh, aye. I did hear that," the other responded.

"I dinna cane who it is, but Sandy said it's women and a young lassie."

"Oh?"

"They must be loaded to be up on the hill. Probably snobby toffs from down south."

Lisa's chest burned with a rush of rage as she stood, a bottle of malbec in one hand and her head bowed as she turned her ear to listen closer.

"It's always the way isn't it?" the other voice responded with a disapproving tone. "Our young anes canna buy property and then you get rich people swooping in buying the big hooses and lording it up."

Lisa grimaced. If only they knew. If they felt the daily grief that gnawed away at her, the guilt, the anguish. All those feelings were the only reason she could afford to "lord it up" on the hill. She would much rather have her parents back than live in that house. If she had a chance to repair the cross feelings, to draw a line under old arguments and move on, she would swap that house in a heartbeat. But they were gone. Wiped out. That house was all she had to show for the lives of her two parents – two hard-working, kind, if a little judgemental and stubborn, people.

Keeping her head bent, not wanting to see who had been talking about the house on the hill, for fear of never being able to speak to them if their paths crossed in the future, which they inevitably would in such a small place, she bought the red wine and dashed straight back to her car as quick as she could.

Pulling into the driveway of their home, a large, proud, sandstone building, she felt relief.

Heather was in the kitchen, peeling potatoes, listening to a comedy podcast, her glossy, black curls pulled back into a ponytail.

"Hey gorgeous," she said, wiping a hand on her starry apron and reaching to pause the episode.

Lisa waved the bottle of wine at her wife before placing it on the counter and walking over to take a long, restorative hug. She didn't want to let go.

After a minute, Heather pulled back and looked deep in Lisa's eyes. "You OK?"

"Yeah, I just overheard some biddies in the shop speculating about us 'toffs' up here," she replied.

"Oh my god, don't let it bother you. People are jealous, that's all. It's human nature. They don't know us, so it's not personal."

Tears pricked at Lisa's eyes and her forehead creased in a tormented frown. "We came up here to get away from people gossiping," she said, exasperation dancing on her words. "I'm sick of it. Why are people even interested in what anyone else is doing?" Her voice broke as tears broke the banks of her eyelids and rolled down her cheeks.

"Come here," Heather said softly, pulling her in for another hug. "It really doesn't matter. Honestly. Who cares what some people in the shop who don't know us think?" She peered into Lisa's eyes and smiled. "OK?"

Lisa sniffed and nodded. "I suppose so." She fiddled with the top of the wine bottle thoughtfully for a few moments, circling it with her index finger, taking time to compose herself.

Then her stomach flipped when she remembered the dolphin encounter and while she cracked open the bottle and poured two glasses of wine, she regaled the whole experience enthusiastically, animating the scene with hand gestures and sound effects. It brought her back to life.

CHAPTER 9 – BRYDIE

"Copy...and...paste," whispered Brydie as she acted out the gestures on her laptop. She was preparing a little booklet about open water swimming safety and recommended gear. Kim had laughed at her when she suggested this, but, ever the cautious one, Brydie insisted she didn't want to be encouraging anyone to plunge into the chilly North Sea without offering a little bit of advice. She was far from an expert, but since putting word out about a possible group for like-minded sea worshippers, she had been obsessively watching videos and reading articles online to swot up on the subject.

The booklet included tips for neoprene boots and gloves at 5mm thick, dry robes, plenty of layers of clothing for afterwards, hot drinks and tips on avoiding after drop.

These north waters would never get much warmer than fourteen to sixteen degrees, even in the hottest months of the ocean's year in Scotland, which, according to the fifth website Brydie examined, were August and September. She was amazed to learn that when a swimmer leaves the water their body continues to cool down and even if they felt fine in the water, they could suffer shivering and even hypothermia half an hour *after* they get out. She pasted tips about getting dressed in layers as quickly as possible and avoiding hot showers for a little while as this could make someone faint with the sudden change in temperature.

It was all quite terrifying for a complete beginner. She tucked away some bags of jelly babies and a blanket in her swim bag - as advised, in case any of her fellow swimmers suffered cold water shock. And finally, she ordered a safety rope online to throw out to anyone who might drift away from the group – heaven forbid.

"You can't buy absolutely everything you see to do with wild swimming," Doug commented, placing one hand on her shoulder affectionately as he passed the breakfast bar where Brydie was tapping away on the keys.

"I know honey," she replied, not even looking up from the screen. "I just want the essentials in case we get into any trouble. I don't want to go out there completely unprepared and be the dumbass that causes a whole heap of drama because we didn't know what we were doing," she added, looking up at him with a grimace. He nodded a seal of approval and continued pouring hot water into his mug. Clutching a steaming mug of coffee, Doug bent to kiss Brydie's head of wild auburn curls and padded back down the hallway in his slippers to his home office.

Zapping noises rung out around the kitchen causing Brydie to jump in her seat as though someone had let off a fog horn in the room. Her heart fluttered quickly. Her phone was usually on silent so its ringtone was like a terribly rude intruder in her life. She glanced at the screen, which said "Mum" and she sighed with relief that it wasn't one of the restaurants she had given her CV to and picked up.

"Hi Mum," she said cheerily.

"Hi darling, just a quick one. Do you like candles?"

Brydie frowned with amusement. "Yes. Everyone likes candles, surely."

"You'd be surprised," her mum, Sally, replied. "The

amount of candles I've had regifted to me by Maureen and Linda, that *I* gave to them... it's ridiculous. *They* obviously don't appreciate a good candle." She tutted and paused, clearly needing a moment to roll her eyes or shake her head. "Anyway," she continued. "I'm in the bargains place just now, I can never remember what it's called."

"Even though you're currently inside it?" Brydie asked, smirking.

Her mum sighed with impatience. "Anyway... what was I saying... oh yes, they have some really good candles here that are less than half price. Not the cheap rubbish ones that leave black marks around the glass, but the really strong smelling ones that come in gorgeous jars with patterns on them. Do you want some?"

Brydie hesitated. "Erm, yes please. I'll give you money for them when I next see you."

"No, no, darling, I know you're not earning anymore, so I'll treat you," Sally said in a hurried tone. "Any news on the job front?"

Brydie pursed her lips with annoyance. "No," she replied curtly.

"You don't want to be *too* dependent on Doug," her mum said with an exasperated tone. "He already has so much hold over you. It's like you've given up on yourself because you've got this older man and you let him take care of *everything*. I don't know *where* you get it from. I've never relied on a man. I wouldn't want one. Bloody pain in the arse, that's all they are."

"Mum. He's my husband. Has been for six years," Brydie said, unable to prevent a little irritation slipping through in her tone. "I haven't given up on myself. I'm working on a project, actually," she said, trying to muster an air of power to her words.

"Oh really?" Sally said, sounding unconvinced. "Is it another craft project?"

Brydie pursed her lips and glanced at the basket of beads and jewellery wire sitting in the corner of the kitchen, untouched for three weeks.

"Maybe," Brydie said meekly.

"Darling," Sally said firmly. "I love your little projects, but you need to be doing something that's going to make you some *actual* money...of your *own*. What if Doug leaves you? You'll be penniless."

"Mum! Doug's not going to leave me. We're fine. And I *am* trying to make money." She sighed and glanced out the window towards the crashing waves, reminding herself to let the words flow over her.

"I mean," Sally continued, "I'd understand if you were at home with young children or cleaning the house all the time, but..."

"Oh, that's not fair," Brydie said, finally snapping. "You know we've been trying for a baby."

"Yes, sweetheart," Sally responded briskly, "and I did warn you at the beginning that the age gap between you and Doug could make fertility tricky, and..."

"I have to stop you there, mum," Brydie interjected. "I wasn't going to tell anyone this yet, but Doug's not the problem. Apparently, it's me."

Silence.

"Oh sweetie," Sally said, her tone softening. "Well, there must be stuff we can do. Herbal things. I'll start researching."

Brydie's whole body stiffened. "No, mum, it's OK. I'm dealing with it. I don't need you to research anything. Honestly. I'm actually OK. Besides we have Lucas and Millie. We *have* a family."

"Well..." Sally said with a long drawn out vowel, "that's not really the same as having your own kids is it? They're only there a couple of times a week. You didn't get to bond with them as babies. In fact, you're too bloody good to them. They walk all over you and he just lets them."

Brydie took a long, deep breath in and closed her eyes. "I thought you were in a hurry at the shop," she said with a questioning tone.

"Yes, I am," Sally said, quickly changing her tone back to urgent. "I've got so much shopping to do and then I have to go and pop by Auntie Val's. I really can't be bothered, but she'll just phone and complain she never sees anyone if I don't pop my head in with some biscuits."

"OK, say hi from me", Brydie replied trying to push her mum off the call as quickly as possible.

When they hung up, Brydie cupped her chin in her hand, supported by her elbow on the kitchen breakfast bar and stared at the ocean view being framed by the window. The waves were calling her in soothing tones that everything was actually OK in that moment. She let out a sigh and turned back to her booklet project. At least there was the first group swim to look forward to later in the week. She'd already had a couple of responses to the post on social media about potential swim buddies. This was something exciting to stamp out the negative thoughts that were creeping around her skull since the phone call. Thoughts of sea swimming shooed them back into their dark, distant corner where they belonged.

"Woolly hats for warmth," Brydie said decisively, reminding herself what would come next on the bullet point list. She smiled at the booklet taking shape on screen – a collection of wise words and little illustrations of dolphins and mermaids. Cheery yet helpful. Just like her.

CHAPTER 10 –
GROUP LAUNCH

"Hey gorgeous!" Kim shrieked, spreading her arms out wide to embrace Brydie, who was struggling under the weight of an enormous beach bag, packed to overflowing. Brydie dumped the bag at her feet and hugged her friend with a stiff, nervous stance.

Brydie pulled back and grimaced in an over the top way and the two women laughed.

"Let's see if anyone actually turns up," Brydie said, rolling her eyes.

The sky was an overcast pale grey under a thick duvet of clouds. The surface of the sea was whipped slightly by a cool breeze, making it look moody as if it was flat out refusing to shimmer and reflect like it had done yesterday on a calm, clear day. Today the ocean was a little less inviting.

The pair stood in silence for a moment, eyes fixed on the horizon, each in deep thought.

"I'm already chilly," Kim said, rubbing her arms which were enclosed in a puffy winter jacket.

"Let's grab a seat," Brydie said decisively and gestured to the worn sandstone wall by the concrete slipway into the water. They dumped their bags and huddled together on a long, smooth stretch of stone, which made for quite a nice natural sofa. It was the perfect height for changing out of shoes and into surf boots – which caused both women to strain and groan and tug until they were tucked in tight to the heat-keeping footwear.

"I'm glad we decided to launch the group from the slappy instead of the beach. It means we can park right at the water instead of walking along the beach to go in way over there," Brydie said, glancing across the water to the beach in the distance.

"Totally," Kim agreed. "Plus, we've got this lovely concrete slope to guide us right into the water. We won't have to take half a beach's worth of sand home on our boots after."

"And I think one of the ladies who's coming has trouble with her hips so this is ideal. Easy access."

Kim screwed up her face before asking: "Why IS it called the slappy?"

Brydie shrugged. "Could be because slappy sounds like slipway...or...look at that..." She pointed to the waves hitting off the stone wall of the esplanade. "That's definitely slapping!"

Kim laughed. "I guess so. It's still a lot calmer at the slappy than over at beach where those massive waves are breaking. It's more like a flat swimming pool here because we're protected by the harbour. I do like a wipeout though, so we'll have to go back to the waves soon. A wee bit of delicious danger."

After a short silence, Kim shifted awkwardly on the wall, turning her body towards Brydie and confided: "Rick's being surprisingly nice, by the way. He wants us to have coffee together to talk about our routine with the kids and 'build bridges' as he put it. Weird. The last time I saw him he was in a bit of a mood with me."

"Hmm," Brydie pondered. "Maybe he's met someone so he wants to move on...?"

"What? Since the other day?" Kim questioned with a smirk. "I doubt it. We'll see what comes of it. He's probably realised there's no going back, so there's no point in making things difficult by being bitter."

The sound of car wheels on gravel snatched the two women out of their conversation and coaxed them to turn their heads to see a red Volvo parking behind them. They eyed each other expectantly.

A woman in a long, black winter anorak got out of the car and spent a minute or two fumbling around in the back seat before pulling out a bulging holdall and slinging it over her shoulder. She looked around and when her eyes fell on Brydie and Kim she smiled nervously and raised her hand in a gentle wave. As she walked over, the two women stood up, smiles spread across their faces like welcome banners.

"Hi, I'm Martha," said the woman, breathless with nervous energy.

They each introduced themselves. "Pop your bag here next to ours," Brydie said, gesturing to the heap of essentials at their feet.

"I'm so nervous," Martha said, suddenly looking a bit pale. "I haven't been swimming in a pool, let alone the sea, for years."

"Ah, don't worry," reassured Kim. "We're not proper swimmers. We just stand around, letting the cold water work its magic and occasionally do a little bit of breast stroke. It's more just a dip than a swim."

"Of course, if you want to do front crawl, that's entirely up to you," Brydie added. "Do it your way. We're just offering company."

Martha laughed. "No, I prefer the sound of the first scenario. A casual dip is plenty for me."

Brydie grinned. "Cool."

Silence fell on the three women as their eyes all transfixed on the petrol-blue, choppy ocean. "I wonder if we'll have anyone else join us," Kim queried gently. "We said ten, and it's about ten past now. We could wait another couple of minutes to give people a chance."

The other two women nodded in agreement.

"Do you have your swimsuit on under there?" Brydie asked, pointing to Martha's thick coat.

"Yes, I'm all suited and ready," Martha said, between shallow breaths. "And I have swim shoes. I'll have to get some of these proper boots," she added, looking at Brydie's black neoprene boots.

"Yeah, they make a huge difference," Brydie enthused. "They're worth the money as they stop your toes going numb."

Kim hopped from foot to foot anxiously, "Yeah, I used these boots for the first time last week and felt so much better. Also, I'm not keen on squelchy sand under my feet and I would freak out if I stood on seaweed or a crab or something."

Martha chuckled. "Yeah, you never know what's under your feet, so I'm glad I have water shoes for now. They won't keep me warm, but they'll stop me getting nipped or hurt on stones at least."

Brydie checked her watch. "OK, let's go for it. It doesn't look like anyone else is coming."

Martha's faced stiffened into a fearful frown. "I'm a bit nervous about baring all," she said, hugging her ribcage tightly. "I keep trying to lose weight, but I just can't do it. I feel yuck just now."

Brydie put one arm around Martha's shoulder. "Please don't even think like that. We're all in it together. Once you're in that water I promise you won't even think about your body. You'll be distracted by...well, the cold!"

Martha let out a hoot of laughter. "You're really selling it to me now," she said sarcastically.

"Focus on what's made you want to do this," Kim added sincerely. "Think of how great you'll feel afterwards."

"Good point," Martha said, sucking in her bottom lip in contemplation. "I want to do this to show myself I *can* do things out of my comfort zone. And I read that it helps aches and pains, and *God* knows I've got *them*."

"Yeah, apparently it really does soothe pain," Brydie agreed with a gentle smile. "Perfect. I'm so glad you're here. This is exactly why we're doing this. So people can get what they need from the experience but have other nutters to do it with for safety."

Martha laughed. "I'm glad I found you nutters then."

She unzipped her padded, waterproof coat with determination and dropped it to the ground, taking a sharp inward breath as her bare skin met with the cool spring breeze. Goosebumps formed on her flesh and she rubbed her arms aggressively.

Brydie let out a whoop of encouragement before throwing her thick, oversized fleece to the ground. "Let the cellulite meet the sea!" she hollered.

"You don't have any," Martha exhaled, now shaking – but whether it was from nerves or the cold was much like the sea that day... unclear.

Brydie began squeezing her outer thigh to emphasise the faint lumps under the surface of her skin and exclaimed, laughing: "Everyone does!"

Kim clutched at her chest, as if offering her bust some armour. She noticed Martha watching and explained: "You could hang your coat off these things! I'm chilly, so they're a bit…menacing."

Martha let out a shriek, like an excited parrot. She seemed to ease suddenly and a smile crept across her lips. "OK ladies," she said with a sudden boldness, "It's now or never."

The three women walked, tentatively, down the slipway which was being lapped at by the sea. With a thick stone wall at one side and the harbour wall lying at a right angle to the slipway, they were walking into a protected corner of the beach, which was level like a swimming pool – offering only small peaks of motion. They could see miles of beach stretching out to the right, showing the contrast of strength as fearsome, white waves clawed at the exposed sand in the distance.

Martha let out a shriek as the water hit her thighs. "Jeepers, that's cold."

"Wait 'til it hits your boiler room," Kim smirked, pointing to Martha's nether region.

Martha laughed and braced herself. As the three women walked further into the water, allowing it to gently envelope them as it gradually deepened all that could be heard were deep breaths and the occasional shriek as a new bit of skin was touched by coolness.

Suddenly, Brydie stretched out her arms and dove forward, allowing her shoulders to go under the water and forming a breast stroke motion. "Wooohoo!" she yelled and turned to the others. "I'm in!"

Martha stood with the water tickling her waist, giving Brydie a thumbs up, while Kim splashed water up her shoulders in preparation to join her friend. She turned to Martha and said: "This really helps me. If I splash myself first, it's not so much of a shock."

"My legs are a bit numb," Martha said with slight

concern.

Brydie, who was now swimming in a circle, turned to face her new acquaintance. "Just wait. In a couple of minutes, I promise you will feel amazing."

"OK, in for a penny, in for a pound," Martha cried and lunged forward, plunging her top half into the chilly water and joining Brydie in the breast stroke game.

The other two women cheered encouragement. "Yes Martha! You're definitely a wild dooker now!"

"I am aren't I?" Martha said with a large dose of surprise and pride.

The three women were no more than bobbing heads as their bodies were emersed in the gently churning water, huge grins on their faces.

Above them, on the stone esplanade that ran alongside the slipway, someone leaned over the metal railing and shouted: "You lot are off your heads! Is it nice in there?"

The bobbing heads all turned in response to see Mike, the postie.

"It's amazing!" Kim called out in reply.

"Blooming freezing!" Martha retorted.

After Mike had laughed and marvelled then moved on, Martha turned to the other swimmers and said, with an air of disbelief: "Brydie, you were right, my skin actually feels lovely now. It's not numb or sore, it's tingling with a sort of... sparkly warmth."

"See? It's beautiful isn't it?" she replied with a satisfied grin. "There's nothing else like it."

A cry from the distance swept across the water and bounced off the corner walls: "Wait for me!"

In confusion, they looked to the esplanade in time to see Ray running towards them waving a stripey towel like a flag.

She got to the slipway, stripped off her kaftan to reveal a canary yellow swimsuit and strode in effortlessly, smiling and declaring: "I saw you from my window. I couldn't miss this!"

"Excellent!" Kim called to her enthusiastically. "I hoped I'd see you again."

Ray beamed. "And this time, I'm clothed...as promised."

Martha frowned in wonder and Ray turned to her and said discreetly: "I did a skinny dip the last time I saw this bathing beauty."

"Oh wow!" Martha said with a laugh. "You're brave."

"Brave....crazy... you pick," Ray said with a mischievous smile.

Ray was already in up to her neck without much of a reaction. Her mustard yellow suit nothing but a blur under the water as she floated on her front, closing her eyes in blissful joy.

A chat about where everyone lived started up, while Ray continued to float in silence. She muttered a few words to herself and then opened her eyes to join the conversation.

"I was just offering my thank yous to the universe and putting out some manifestations for the future too. You'll get used to that, I'll be doing it every time," Ray said softly, as if her time with her eyes closed had transported her into a different place and she was taking her time to emerge back to reality.

"I think that's wonderful," Kim said, with a look of admiration. "I might get into that too. This water does something to me. I actually cried the first time I got in."

"Did you?" Brydie asked in shock.

"Yeah," Kim replied looking at her friend sincerely. "I

didn't say anything, but it was as if I really needed to let it all out and this was the only place that felt right to do it."

Brydie gave her friend a warm smile which sent hidden signals of support and love and the smile on the receiving end was a signal that they had been well and truly received.

Suddenly, Brydie's expression changed. "We'd better not stay in too long. It's only about eight degrees."

Martha nodded, "It's my first time, too, so I'd better not push it."

Brydie, Martha and Kim began breast stroking back towards the slipway.

"I'll grab another minute," Ray called after them as she turned over gracefully to float on her back, gazing at the overcast sky.

The next ten minutes were a struggle of wriggling out of wet boots, attempts at removing soggy swimsuits without flashing any unsuspecting villagers – a feat which was only *just* accomplished by two of the group. Martha inadvertently flashed a wet bottom towards the cottages, before realising and whipping her towel behind her. "I really need to get one of these changing jackets," she said meekly. "Brogie doesn't need to see my enormous butt."

The laughter kept them going during the tugging and heaving, until eventually all three were dressed and wrapped up in jackets, sipping a mixture of chai tea, coffee and hot chocolate from their separate flasks.

Brydie handed out the advice leaflets to the others, looking a little embarrassed. "I know it's really nerdy," she said, "but I thought it was important we all know the same stuff if we're going to be doing this regularly."

Martha smiled enormously. "That's the nicest thing

ever," she reassured Brydie. "I don't know enough about the safety of all this, so you are an absolute star."

Brydie grinned with a relieved confidence. "Thanks. I might see if the guys from the coastguard unit at the harbour will give us a little talk once we're established and maybe have more people joining us."

"Fab idea," Kim chimed in. "I know Gordon from the coastguard. His kid goes to school with Gigi. I can ask him if you like. Or pass on your number." Her expression changed from light joy to a serious frown. "I'd better nip off as I start work in an hour. It'll be the busy spell too – lunchtime."

"It's always busy in there," Brydie commented. "I might pop in for coffee later actually. I could do with one of their scones."

Kim smiled. "OK, I'll keep you a really nice one behind the counter. That's my superpower...the ability to stash cakes."

"Good superpower," Brydie replied throwing a fist in the air, exclaiming: "Scone power!"

Ray strolled casually up the slipway, water dripping from her limbs as she squeezed her bright red locks to dry them slightly.

"That was fabulous," she said in a breathy, contented tone. "When's the next dip?"

Brydie shrugged and looked at the others. "Shall we start our own page for the group on social media and that way we can post times and suggestions for swims?"

They all agreed it was the best plan with nods of approval and smiles as their bodies tingled with the all encompassing effects from being emerged in cool water.

"My skin feels like it's buzzing with an electric current," Martha said with a huge grin.

"It's amazing," Ray agreed. "There's nothing like it."

They went their separate ways: Kim to work at the village coffee shop, Brydie to prepare for her step kids coming to stay for the rest of the week, Martha to grab the last few hours of peace before an evening shift at the hospital and Ray to her den of zen where time had little meaning and stress was a long forgotten word.

The Brogie Bay Dookers had completed their maiden voyage and then departed on land with serene smiles and tingling bodies. And they were already looking forward to their next hug from the ocean.

CHAPTER 11 – MIKE

Bubbles drifted slowly upwards in the golden liquid in Mike's glass as he stroked the rim thoughtfully. The beer was giving him a warm, melting feeling as it hit the spot, softening the edges of his mind.

Folk guitar riffs drifted softly from the speakers in the corner of his small living room. His eyes were fixed on his glass, staring, while his mind went elsewhere.

It was his eldest daughter's twenty-fifth birthday. He picked up his phone again to check for messages. Nothing. He opened the texts mailbox to read what he'd written again…for the fifth time.

Happy birthday darling.
Are you doing anything nice?
Did you get my card and money?
Hope they arrived safely.

Four messages in a row. Spread out in increments of half hours. No responses. He looked at the clock. It was only tea time, she would probably reply later, he decided, not losing hope.

Katie, his daughter, got married three months ago. Didn't even tell Mike. He only found out when he saw his mother – Katie's grandmother, obviously – had posted a few pictures on social media of the big day. After the initial reaction of gut-wrenching hurt at not knowing his daughter had walked down the aisle without him, he immediately ran out to the post office to buy a card and put money in it to send to the happy couple. There had been no response, no thank you, for the gift.

He considered the possibility that maybe his daughter had moved house, but after a phone call to his mum that theory was put to bed. She was still at the same address. He temporarily concluded that there were surely problems with the mail at this end and that his thank you card must have got misplaced in a sorting office somewhere. Eventually, Mike accepted that she just didn't care. She didn't want contact. He wasn't ready to give up though. Soon, there could be grandkids. He knew it was worth casting his rod every now and then in case there might eventually be a bite, however little the catch might end up being.

Finally, he peeled his gaze away from the lava-lamp-esque movement of bubbles in beer and glanced out of the full-length glass doors which framed a small balcony overlooking the bay. The room was barely bigger than a car, but it was enough for him. He bought it after leaving the forces. This was his 'The End' home. The home that would see him through his older years, he hoped. Band posters and bits and pieces of wooden wall art picked up from his travels adorned the walls, making him feel like he belonged in that tiny space.

He watched intently through the glass doors as birds swooped and dove into the water beyond his balcony, catching their evening meal.

Food. What would *he* have? He thrust his head back and rubbed his weary face. Everything felt like an effort all of a sudden. He'd rather open a packet of crisps and another beer than move to the kitchen to cook anything. What would be the point? No-one was there to criticise or comment anyway. Crisps and beer would suffice.

He picked up his phone again and searched for his mother in contacts. It rung out. No answer.

The evening dragged in slowly, filled by a documentary on Jimi Hendrix and a few more beers.

Through a slight beer haze, Mike lost concentration on the band on screen. He wasn't taking in any facts or anecdotes anymore. He checked his phone again. Still no replies.

A burning surge of frustration pushed upwards from the pit of his belly and into his throat. He began typing.

You are heartless. I've spent years trying so hard to reach out. I send you money. I ask how you are. I call. I text. I wait and wait and wait and nothing. I tried to be there for you when you were younger but your mother was a...

Changing his mind in a flash of clarity, Mike launched his phone across the room, startling at the clatter it made as it hit the wooden door frame.

His heart was pounding firmly in his ribcage, reminding him he was very much alive and basically a carcass full of emotion. He shook his head and stroked his beard. No good would come of sending a brutally honest text. He'd been in this very position, on this very sofa, many a time. He always deleted the text. Never sent it. He would never come out on top of this family battle, he knew it. Bridges had been burnt to a cinder long ago. He tried to live in the now. He even had a bloody tea towel to show for it that said: "All we have is now". He couldn't keep reliving this torturous guilt over and over. He vowed to himself to keep moving forward as he downed the last sip of beer and switched off the TV, becoming intensely aware of the sudden silence in his flat.

His stomach rumbled, breaking the silence and reminding him he had barely eaten that night.

He moved through to his equally tiny bedroom and lay in the dark, cool sheets, listening to the swishing movement of the sea back and forth through his slightly open window. The continual sound of foamy water breaking on sand and rocks was comforting. It lifted him from his own thoughts, which were relentlessly heavy and self-critical, and allowed him to picture the wider world outside his dark walls. He felt insignificant next to that mass of powerful water that never gave up on its duty day or night.

Before long he settled into a restorative sleep, which blanked his mind and reset him.

The next morning, Mike was out with his mail cart, like a new tide repeating the same loop of duty. He took a deep breath of sea air and enjoyed that familiar scent of salt and seaweed, plus a fishy mist coming from the boats in the harbour. He took a quick glance into the main body of the harbour to look for Sammy Seal who was more often than not lolling around in the oily, industrial water like an over-indulged medieval king full of food and revered by his subjects – who were every single human who passed the harbour and all the fishermen who would chuck him slops every now and then.

Mike gave Sammy a salute, muttered "what a life" then began heading towards the row of sea-facing cottages.

Before he got to Brenda's carefully preened garden, he heard shrieks coming from down in the water. He stopped pushing the cart suddenly, alert, in listening mode. Another shriek rang out.

Bloody hell, he thought urgently, *someone's fallen over the esplanade railing and into the water.* Abandoning his mail, he dashed to the railing to lean over and check out the emergency situation. But there was no emergency to be seen. Just three women laughing and yelling as they embraced the cold water. A rush of relief flowed through him like a powerful wave.

He called out to the group that they must be off their heads. There was a chilly breeze and the water looked a little choppy and very uninviting. He wouldn't let on that he had panicked and was preparing to call the coastal rescue team, that wouldn't be cool.

He recognised them all – that was the blessing of his job. The one with the red suit was Gordon Street, the black suit lady lived up on Seabird Rise and the pink suit, hmmm, he had to think for a moment, ah, yes, she was also on Gordon Street, but she barely answered her door, that's why he struggled to place her.

He watched for a minute, envious of the evident joy they were oozing, and in awe of their bravery. He'd been in this sea on one of the hottest days in summer a few years back and even in those temperatures he felt as though his man parts were going to shrivel up and drop off. He shuddered at the thought.

Better stop watching, he thought, *you'll look like a pervert*. Yet it was hard to peel his eyes away from the cluster of pure happiness. It was intriguing.

Turning around to go back to his cart, knowing he should never have left it unattended, he was met with an unusual sight that stopped him dead.

Ray was running across the greenie – a patch of grass that separated the esplanade from the cottages – waving a towel above her head. The towel trailed behind her in the breeze, making her look like a heroine going into battle. Yet, there was a lightness about her face as she ran. It was decorated with such a delicate smile that Mike found himself staring, open-mouthed. She had on a multi-coloured ankle-length dress that whipped and whooshed around her lean legs as she sprinted forward and her red hair flicked backwards like dancing flames.

She noticed Mike and shot him a mischievous smile and threw a short "Hi" his way, but kept her momentum, as she was clearly on a mission.

Mike's heart quickened. "Are you going in the sea too?" he called after her, but she was so focussed on joining the joy she hadn't noticed. He felt a little silly, like when he held his hand up for a high five at the depot with Brian the other day and was left hanging for just a moment too long that the high five just felt like a pity one in the end.

The quickening of his heart and open-mouthed gawping hadn't gone unnoticed by Mike and as he walked back to his cart with his hands in his pockets and head bent, he laughed to himself. He clearly had a crush on the most exuberant character in Brogie Bay. She just had something about her.

She's way out of your league, he thought. *She's a free spirit, you're an ex forces dude with too many issues. She's gorgeous, you're...not.* He laughed. *Get a grip.*

CHAPTER 12 – KIM

"**S**o," Kim said, trying to sound less tense than she actually was. "What was it you wanted to talk about?"

Up until this point, she had done so well at avoiding eye contact with Rick. But now that they were sat opposite each other at a tiny square table in the Beach Hut Café where Kim worked, she couldn't exactly maintain her icy power move. She glanced into his dark brown eyes, trying to get a sense of his mood, or rather, his agenda.

He smiled softly and tugged gently at his dark beard. "Listen," he said, tentatively. "I'm sorry I was a bit abrupt the other day. I just want us to go forward being friends... for the kids' sake, you know?"

Kim, pursed her lips in thought. "Oh. Is that it?" she asked, letting a laugh tinge the last word. "I had no idea what this could be about. I thought you either wanted more access to the kids, or *less*, or you'd met someone, or..."

Rick laughed. "No, baby, er, sorry, I shouldn't call you that anymore. No, I just didn't like the way we left things the other day."

He tilted his head to the side and examined her face. It felt all too familiar. Kim's tummy flipped with hot energy. *What the hell? Why am I getting all giddy? He's a dick head. Keep it together.*

"OK. Great," was all she could muster. "Absolutely. We need to be the grown-ups here and show the kids that they can still have positive vibes from both of us...

between both of us."

Rick nodded in agreement before taking a sip from his cappuccino then wiping the froth from the hair on his upper lip. He picked up his tea spoon and began tapping it awkwardly on the saucer, keeping his eyes on the spoon to saucer action, and asked: "What time do you finish here?"

Kim was suddenly flustered. "Erm." She looked around, as if reminding herself where she was and why. Work. "I've got an hour left. Why?"

"Want to collect the kids from school together and go back to yours? Show them we can do it? We can be friends?"

Kim swallowed hard. "I don't see why not," she said, patting down her apron to keep her hands busy, in an attempt to look unflustered. "That's not a bad idea."

At the school gates, they waited side by side. Kim could feel Meghan's eyes on them, clearly trying to piece together why they were both there *together.* Meghan's daughter was in Gigi's class. They had a large house one street away from the school and what appeared – from the outside anyway – to be the perfect little existence. Hubby earned a wad of cash in property development and she had a little side hustle making flower wreaths (well, she *called* it a side hustle, but if it's your only hustle then can it *really* be on the side? On the side of *what*? Kim used to mutter these kinds of thoughts to herself regularly, seeing right through Meghan's pretence of being "flat out" with orders).

A door swung open and a fraught-looking young nursery teacher began eyeing the adults who were scattered across the playground suspiciously, as if her job was actually in government intel trying to stop kidnappings, not teaching children how to chop up their own banana at snack time to promote independence.

A few children ran at their adults before Stan was next in line. He spotted Kim first and the government agent slash teacher waved at her and allowed him to bomb it towards his mum like a clumsy goat kid, all bounce and toothy grin. When his little body slammed into her legs at force, he turned to see his father by her side. "Dad?" he questioned, excitedly, as though he'd just caught Santa Clause in the living room.

"Hey buddy," Rick said gently before bending to scoop him up for a mid-air hug.

Kim couldn't help but watch with a nostalgic glaze spreading across her. This was what she had always wanted. She wanted her kids to be scooped up by their dad into his safe arms. She wanted Meghan to see this and take note that they, too, could have gorgeous family moments and weren't actually a "broken home" as she'd heard Meghan whisper once at the Christmas nativity as Gigi walked on stage as the angel Gabriel and waved at Kim, who was sitting alone amid a sea of couples.

Gigi came out a few minutes later, in a much less energised fashion. She stomped slowly towards her family, looking tired, her eyes darting from Kim to Rick then back again several times.

"You're both here?" she asked, squinting. Then she shrugged and muttered "That's never happened before," before turning to her mum and querying: "Did you get me any leftovers from the cake counter at work? I'm starving."

Kim winced. "No, cookie. I totally forgot. I was in a bit of a hurry to finish today." She could feel her face grow hot with embarrassment at, A – forgetting to bring a snack for the walk home, which was their ritual; and B – being put right off her daily routine by a flaming MAN.

"Never mind," Kim continued, "we'll get something yummy at home. Dad's coming with us."

Gigi looked up at her mum quizzingly.

"Because we're friends," Kim added, knowing Gigi had a thousand questions tugging at her mature brain.

Back at the house, Gigi grabbed a jam sandwich and took it off to her room to draw and listen to music. Stan climbed on top of his dad like a baby monkey while they sat at the kitchen table listening to the aggressive bubbling of water in the kettle while Kim searched for mugs and a jar of coffee.

"So you're not obsessed with that posh coffee machine anymore?" Rick asked, with a hint of smugness.

Kim sighed. "No. It's too expensive. Especially as I'm only part-time at the Beach Hut. Instant will have to do." She waved the jar at him with an over the top smile, enjoying her display of hardship. It felt like she was proving she could do this. She could make sacrifices to keep her ship afloat.

"Fine, that'll do the job," he said supportively before turning Stan upside down and tickling his tummy.

"Go and put on the TV sweetie," Kim said to their son as soon as he was upright again. "Here's a bowl of cookies and apple slices. I'll bring you a drink soon."

"Yummy," he declared and raced through to the living room shouting "I wanna watch the fing about the dog!"

"He's so good with the TV these days," Kim said to Rick. "He finds all the programmes himself."

Rick nodded. "Yeah, I *do* have them part of the week. He does that at mine."

Kim nodded, feeling herself blush a little. Of course he

knew what the kids were capable of.

"What are those for?" Rick asked, pointing to her surf boots and gloves drying on a laundry hanger over the radiator.

Kim swallowed. "I've taken up wild swimming," she answered with forced confidence.

Rick snorted. "What, in the sea? Down there? At this time of year?"

"Yes," she responded firmly with a proud grin. "It's amazing. It leaves your skin all tingly and I've met some new friends through it. It's the best thing I've done in a long time."

He raised his eyebrows. "Well, I think it's crazy, people throwing themselves in the freezing North Sea, but each to their own!" He laughed. "If you're enjoying it…fair play to you." His eyes fixed on her and his tone changed. "Just be careful. Don't get out of your depth. You don't ever go alone do you?"

She smiled. "No. I never go alone. And I always like to know I can touch the sand. I stay shallow enough to be able to stand if I need to."

She turned back round to face the counter and concentrated on spooning granules into their mugs, then suddenly she was aware of a presence at her back. Rick's arm slipped around her waist to her stomach. His soft beard grazed her exposed neck and his warm breath sent shivers down her spine. She froze on the spot, unsure how to respond.

Rick whispered in her ear: "We could have so much, you know. We don't have to throw it away. We were amazing once. We have these beautiful kids."

He kissed her neck and Kim noticed her arms tingled with goosebumps. Still, she stood silently, eyes closed to the scenario.

"I mean it Kimmy," he continued in a breathy, hushed voice. "You're the best woman I've ever known. You loved me once. We were so cool."

She put down the spoon and turned around to face him. Big mistake. Their eyes locked and a rush of familiar lust cursed through every part of Kim's body. They *were* really cool together once. She couldn't deny that. They were arty and edgy and the envy of loads of their friends. They wanted these kids so badly. They wanted the whole shebang – family, house, rock and roll lifestyle. It just didn't add up correctly when it actually happened. It hadn't been fun, or arty, at all.

Rick's face was now so close to hers she could smell the faint lingering mint from the chewing gum he'd had on the walk home from school.

"What if we made a mistake splitting up?" he asked, almost breathless now – his lips but a centimetre from hers.

Still Kim couldn't utter a word. Her heart was pounding fast, her head felt like lava was coursing through it, making a swooshing pulse noise in her ears.

Rick edged a centimetre closer, allowing his lips to brush hers suggestively. His hand tightened around her waist, pulling her as close as she could physically get. "You're so hot," he whispered, his lips grazing hers with each word.

Kim gasped. His skin, his beard, it was all so familiar, so comforting in a way.

As he nuzzled into her neck, whispering sentences about her beauty, her mind wandered. *It would be so much easier if we had one bloody home for the kids. A family unit. Maybe his drinking and smoking aren't so bad these days.*

Maybe he's grown up since the split – seen that he needs to step it up, to actually show up for us all. This would be such a relief. I wouldn't have to do this alone. And I've always fancied him. He's my guy.

Before any other thoughts could creep in to balance the argument, Kim found herself responding with her lips on his, the familiar taste giving her reassurance.

Rick's hand moved down to squeeze her bum and he slipped her some hot tongue. She met it with hers. They knew exactly what to do. They'd been on this fairground ride many a time.

She grabbed the back of his head with her hands and pulled his face ever closer as if to seal some kind of a deal with her lips pressed hard against his. It was all systems go. Her body was responding as it always had – tingling, melting, preparing. She found it reassuring that her organs were still capable of responding in such ways…it had been a while.

Suddenly, they heard footsteps on the wooden floor in the hallway, and with it being a tiny cottage, that meant that any second now the kitchen door would be pushed open. They separated abruptly and Kim turned back to the coffee mugs as if she was fixated on the task.

Stan entered and held out his hand pleadingly. "You said I could have a drink mummy."

"Oh yes, of course. Mummy was busy making coffee. Here we go," she said, as she grabbed a plastic cup from the draining board and started running the cool tap. Rick was standing in front of the juice cupboard. She couldn't look him in the eye. "Could you, please, grab the juice from there?" she asked awkwardly, looking everywhere but his face.

Rick fumbled around in the cupboard before producing

the bottle of pink liquid and Kim tried not to enjoy the feeling too much of having another adult around.

With juice in hand, Stan stomped back down the hallway happily – creating tiny puddles all the way as his juice rocked back and forth in his wobbly grasp.

Kim finally poured hot water into the mugs, stirred, added milk – holding her breath most of the time – and then sat down at the table. She sighed and buried her face in her hands. When she emerged from her hands, she laughed and said directly to Rick: "What does this mean? What just happened?"

He shrugged. "I don't know. I just know that we're too good to give up on."

She couldn't help but smile as she cradled her steaming mug.

After a brief silence, she said: "You seem... different. More positive."

He nodded. "I am. I've had time to work some things out. I know what I want."

Kim's breath felt very shallow in her chest. She was nervous. Excited. Hopeful.

"Well... what happens next?" she asked.

"Let's take it really slow," he said, stroking the handle of his mug. "I'll go back to my place. You carry on here. I'll see you...tomorrow?"

Kim nodded. "OK. It's worth a try. Let's not get our hopes up."

Rick's gaze bore into her, with a mischievous smile tugging at the corners of his lips. It was the kind of smile that had always led to adventure between the two of them. Their relationship before kids had been far from dull. And Kim missed that feeling of being an adult capable of anything. A sexy woman who would sneak about in graveyards with her lover. An artist, who would force her man to pose nude. A vibrant, relevant, grown-ass woman. Maybe, just maybe, she could still be that person.

CHAPTER 13 – RAY

Sitting crossed legged on her colourful, but threadbare, dhurrie rug in the centre of her cluttered living room, Ray's eyes were closed to the world. She listened to seagulls crying in the distance, to the gentle ticking of the kitchen clock (she would *never* have one in the living room. "I don't want to know how much time is slipping away while I'm relaxing," was her stance on that when asked by visitors). The only other sound was the light fluttering of wings and scratching of claws in the bird feeder attached to her living room window as tiny sparrows drove their beaks into the pile of mixed seed, jerking their heads to spray seed onto the window ledge for their mates to enjoy. A gentle smile curled at the edge of Ray's lips to hear this familiar feast.

Her living room was a monument to the living – to her life. Artefacts from around the world adorned each wall – in fact, there was barely any wall space left, so it was just as well Ray's days of roaming were over for the time being. At only sixty, she still wanted to see several countries, but with her pot of gold inheritance money dwindling away slowly, travel didn't seem quite so tempting. She took great care of her body with yoga and good, natural food – she wanted to live a long time – so she needed to make her money last a few decades.

Thinking about wellness, Ray opened one eye and squinted at the ashtray on the polished log side table by her favourite slouchy armchair. There was a stubbed-out joint resting, wearily, in the dish. *The smoking has to stop,* she concluded inwardly. *I don't want to get more wrinkles than necessary. I'll have to start bloomin' baking more. It's just such a faff. But I am good at it. Oh man, that means I'll have to go shopping for ingredients. Sod that. I'll smoke this week...and then I'm done. For sure.*

With her eyes still closed, she took in a deep, slow, breath and sensed the faint aroma of the ocean through her slightly open window. *Who needs world travel when I have this?*

A new sound stole her serenity. It was a vehicle door shutting with a thud at the far end of the street – a familiar sound, which happened at almost the same time every day. Mike. It must be him parking his van and loading the trolley with mail. She opened her eyes and patted down her cotton maxi dress, as if to check she was actually clothed.

She rolled onto her knees then slowly pulled herself to her feet, stretching her arms above her head, enjoying the feeling of teasing out her muscles and ligaments. After a quick glance in the mirror to inspect her tousled hair, she padded, bare foot, through to the kitchen – a little jingling sound ringing out from the bells on her ankle chain.

She filled the kettle with tap water and put it on the aga top to boil. It would hopefully be hot enough by the time Mike reached her house. After the help he had given her by fixing the dodgy front door handle, she wanted to repay him somehow.

Ray stood still for a moment, eye to eye with her twenty-two-year-old self in a picture frame on the wall. In the photograph she was standing outside Jackson's Row registry office in Manchester, wearing a long, cream cotton dress, with a flower headband as her crowning glory. Her first wedding.

She sighed, looking at her younger self, remembering the rush of adrenaline when she said "I do". That picture was taken the day they got married in secret. Neither she, nor Bart Hansen, told their parents about the union until afterwards. They simply dragged a couple of Bart's band mates along as witnesses, did the deed, then piled straight into the local pub.

To Ray, that was pure romance. She didn't care for elaborate weddings that cost more than a car or a trip to the other side of the world. And she certainly didn't care for catering to the wishes of *other people* in order to become man and wife. Expensive set meals, thousand-pound photographers, dresses that cost an unthinkable amount of money. Ray never understood the wedding industry. Which is why she had only ever accepted an invitation to one such wedding in her life. In the nineties she went to a friend's country manor nuptials and was so sickened by the expenditure she gracefully declined every invitation since.

Her moral high ground when it came to wedding budgets said nothing about her endurance for marriages, however. She was only 'Mrs Hansen' for a few months. Their relationship was one that would have killed them had it gone on any longer than that. The arguing, the drinking, the constant road-tripping, Bart's drugs... Looking at the photograph to this day filled Ray with an intense mix of feelings from joy at the memory of being young and in love, to heartbreak at having to walk out of a sordid scene in Ireland after their final fall-out where she had screamed that he was a Class A arsehole after finding him passed out with a naked groupie. Later, Ray had wondered how she was going to divorce Bart when she didn't even know how to contact him, but then word came through that he'd died of an alleged overdose in Texas, of all places. *Problem solved*, was all Ray could think coldly at the time.

Despite these feelings, Ray still liked the picture hanging on the wall. She wasn't ashamed of her experiences, however grim or irresponsible. She often told younger people to really live life – to open themselves up. What would be the point in being scared to divert from 'normal' living? The thought of living a life that consisted of school, job, husband, kids, maintain this forever, retire then die made her shudder. What about the rest of it? The drama, the joy, the wonder, the messy bits?

Her mother had once said to her in a rare moment where they sat together over teacups and bite-size fancies in Ray's late teens: "You know, not everyone craves drama. Some people crave security. Life's riches can be found in the smallest of things."

Ray finally understood that sentiment, in her own way, as she lived out her days in her tiny cottage, worshipping the sea and her treasured artefacts. She really was finding riches in small things these days. But it had taken her decades of movie-worthy adventures to arrive at this point.

She fumbled about in the kitchen drawer and smeared on some tinted beeswax lip balm, which brought some rosy colour to her face and made her eyes twinkle even more. Next to the lip balm in the drawer was a bottle of perfume she'd bought from a catalogue a while back because she really liked young Kate who travelled the village door to door selling beauty products. Ray took to people very quickly if she recognised a kindness in them that deserved nurturing. Ever since then, whenever Kate appeared with a new catalogue, Ray vowed to buy something and support her. Kate would often come in for a mug of coffee during her round and listen to Ray's stories about her life or use Ray as a listening ear for her troubles. They had even meditated together on the living room floor. Ray was a lover of people – not particularly a lover of beauty products, but if it helped out a young woman trying to make ends meet, she would happily snap up some 'smellies'. Ray examined the bottle of perfume and read aloud: "Soft iris and basil...OK." She pumped a few mists of the fragrance towards her neck and wafted it through the air with her hands.

No harm in making the most of myself, she mused.

The kettle began to murmur as heat jiggled its way through the particles of water. Ray gave it a little nod of approval and brought out a tray of flapjack she'd baked the day before – containing only straight-up, sensible ingredients, of course.

She fumbled in the cupboard for two side plates, holding the door with her hip at the same time to stop it collapsing.

Her kitchen was the epitome of shabby chic. It was falling apart, yet at the same time charming with delicate pastel colours, jars of fresh flowers, hanging plants and various candles dotted around.

Her letterbox clattered as mail was gently pushed through.

"Mike," Ray enthused and rushed through to the hallway, opening the door just moments after the delivery.

"Hi Mike," she breathed joyfully. "How are you today?"

Mike looked startled as he turned back to face the door. "Oh, hi, you're bright and breezy today," he said, struggling to make eye contact.

"Yeah, I've been on the go for hours," she replied. "Listen, I really appreciate you fixing the door," she said, rubbing the edge of its frame. "I wondered if you wanted a quick coffee and snack…to say thank you."

She eyed him with an air of uncertainty.

Mike fiddled with his pockets and shifted his weight from foot to foot, as if searching for the answer. Eventually, he stumbled across the words: "Well, OK, I have five minutes. That would be nice."

He entered the hallway, glancing at all the artwork on the wall as he moved towards the living room. "Wow, you've got a really interesting place," he said softly, mesmerised by art.

Ray laughed. "In a good way?"

Mike cleared his throat and responded quick as a flash: "Oh yeah, of course. It's all the art. You have great taste. Are these original paintings?"

He leaned forward to examine a framed picture of a woman in a brightly-coloured wrap dress with a small child on her hip.

"No, no," Ray said, shaking her head. "Just a print. But I got it in India. It reminds me of being there…there was a woman just like that whose little boy was a darling and used to hug me every time I walked by."

Mike nodded, impressed. "Did you live there?"

Ray paused, considering the question. "I spent a couple of months roaming around there, in my thirties, with a boyfriend. We ended up working on a settlement for a few weeks where Americans had set up a sort of meditation retreat. It was great, but Derek – the boyfriend – had to get back to London so we couldn't stay."

Mike swallowed. "You've certainly had some adventures," he said looking at Ray with wide eyes.

"Oh, honey, you don't know the half of them," Ray responded with a flirtatious giggle. She continued: "You don't strike me as being afraid of an adventure yourself." Mike sighed. "I guess not. I've done a bit of travelling. Just holidays, mind you. And time in different countries with the air force."

Ray nodded and smiled. "See. You're a man of the world. I knew it."

He laughed nervously.

"Anyway," Ray said, sensing it was time to shift the mood, for poor shy Mike, "about that coffee. Take a seat and I'll be right back."

Mike cautiously settled himself into a saggy armchair by the fireplace. He slunk backwards into the welcoming bosom of cushions, then changed his mind and sat upright abruptly. He placed his hands in his pockets. Changed his mind and moved them onto his lap. He was stiff and fidgety.

Ray appeared from the kitchen with a tray and placed it down on the side table.

"What do you take in yours?" she asked, meeting his gaze and noticing him throwing his glance away instantly.

"Just milk," he replied quickly.

Ray smirked as she stirred the hot liquid. She'd seen men act this way many a time.

"Here you go," she said, handing him a rustic pottery mug and a small plate with a wedge of flapjack.

Mike sat back in his chair and seemed to ease with his first sip of coffee.

Ray sat on the sofa, aware of leaving enough space between them to make sure he felt at ease. A smile of comfort and satisfaction spread across her face as she cradled her mug and sniffed the steam. "I love the smell of coffee," she said, glancing at Mike. "It brings back feelings of coffee shops the world over – that feeling of indulgence – a moment to just be."

Mike nodded. He took a bite of flapjack and his expression changed. "This is lovely," he said. "Where did you get it?"

"I made it," Ray said, as if stating the obvious. "My secret is local honey. It adds a touch of gold."

Mike stopped chewing suddenly, and with a look of uncertainty asked: "It doesn't have…any other *special* ingredients does it?"

Ray threw her head back in laughter. "Oh my god, Mike. Do you mean weed?"

He nodded.

"I'm not *that* bad," she exclaimed. "I would never just serve up hash cakes for a guest without asking them. That's for special occasions, or in my case, Wednesdays, Fridays and Sundays."

His eyes widened and Ray let out an illicit giggle. "Kidding. I don't restrict myself to those days. Why would I?"

The pair sipped and chewed quietly for a moment before Ray leaned forward eagerly and said: "Oh, that day I ran past you on the green, I was going wild swimming with a bunch of fabulous women."

"Yeah, I spotted them just before you joined them," he said with an amused expression. "It's not even summer weather yet. I don't know how you all cope in that water."

Ray closed her eyes and smiled. "It's sublime. Honestly. The sharp bite of chill when your skin first meets the water is like electric shock therapy…"

"Exactly," Mike guffawed. "You wouldn't catch me

doing it."

"Really?" Ray asked, suddenly eyeing him intensely. "Not even for the pure bliss that comes just after the shock. Your skin adjusts after a few minutes and you find yourself buzzing all over, gently. I swear it's addictive."

Mike pursed his lips as he considered the facts. "I mean, that does sound great. I guess it's the old phrase – no pain, no gain."

Ray nodded tentatively. "Something like that."

"Well, I'd have to wear a wetsuit until the height of summer," Mike added.

"Sure," Ray said, nodding, as if they'd made an agreement. "Whatever works for you. It's all about embracing nature and allowing yourself to let go. If you need to wrap yourself in neoprene to do that, who the hell cares?"

Mike looked nervous, suddenly. "I didn't mean…I mean I suppose…"

"Do you have a wetsuit?" Ray quizzed.

"Yes."

"Well then. You should join us. Feel the sea envelope you in its giant hug," she said leaning towards him more, imploring him to say yes.

Mike, put his mug down on the little table. "Maybe," he said, shaking his head and laughing. "I'll think about it."

He stood up. "Well, thanks for the coffee, that was so nice. I'd better get back to work."

"No problem," Ray responded, getting up to stand with him. "It's the least I could do, after your fix-it job."

They walked silently to the front door. As Mike's foot hit the step outside, he turned and smiled awkwardly. "Bye then."

Ray nodded with a smile and closed the door gently

behind him. She moved through to the living room, suddenly aware of the silence and looked over at his empty mug with a smile. It has been nice to share some time. There was something really calming about his presence. No bravado. No ego. Just calmness.

CHAPTER 14 – MARTHA

The velvety notes of Motown classics filled the kitchen as Martha strutted back and forth to the fridge, wiggling her hips as she went. The fan oven whirred in the background adding an extra layer to the sound.

Martha weighed out cocoa powder, bending to be eye level with the scales, ensuring she was following the brownie recipe to the gram.

As she folded the powder into the mix with a lime green spatula, she sang the lyrics to Marvin Gaye's 'What's Goin' On?' under her breath and trailing behind by a few seconds as she copied what she heard, having forgotten all the words.

Ron appeared at the kitchen door, draped in a navy dressing gown with a thin layer of grey stubble accentuating his gruff, tired ensemble.

"What you up to?" he asked, attempting to peer over Martha's shoulder. She was dressed already, despite it only being first thing on a Saturday morning and neither of them having work to go to.

"I'm baking brownies to take to the next swim," Martha said excitedly, letting a grin take over her face. "We warm up with hot drinks afterwards, so I thought – why not make a tasty piece to add to the fun?"

"Ooh, I love it when you make brownies," Ron responded, looking part enthusiastic, part dismayed. "Will there be any for us? Will I get some?"

Martha laughed at his pleading expression and rolled

her eyes. "Yes. I've made a double batch so you can have some. And I'm going to take some up to mum and dad's. I'm a bit worried about them at the moment," she added, her stance stiffening and a frown shattering her previous amused expression. "Obviously, dad's losing the plot and not able to do much anymore, but I'm starting to worry that mum's forgetting both their medication at times. The other day I was there, I asked about it and she got really cross, saying I was patronising her and that she may be in her late eighties but she's not stupid."

Ron grimaced. "Have you spoken to the carer about it?"

"No," Martha replied, looking fraught. "I'm going to have to sneak her phone number from the notebook on mum's hallway table so I can start having these kinds of conversations. It used to be that mum was so capable she could take care of them both, but I think it's having an effect on her now. She's changed. She called me Barbara the other day."

"Who the hell's Barbara?" Ron asked, his eyebrows shooting upwards.

"Her sister," Martha said with a hint of disapproval, "who died decades ago. She was much older than mum, so I never really got to know her as an auntie, which is why you've rarely heard of her. But it's like Barbara keeps popping back into mum's mind. And now I'm reminding her of her."

There was a pause in conversation for a moment as the couple allowed those thoughts to sink in and separately ponder their weight and worth. The whizzing fan of the oven and the gentle music from the small speaker on the windowsill took centre stage once more.

"Anyway," Martha said, breaking through the kitchen soundtrack, "I'm going to pop by innocently later with these cakes to spy on them and check if they're keeping on top of things. Lord knows I don't want to move them in here with us, but what if they're not safe on their own anymore?"

Ron folded his arms and made a pained expression. "I know. It's a relief for me that my mum still has all her marbles in her nineties. She's amazing," he said softly. "Can you imagine if we had to look after her. There's no way we could have her move in with us. She'd be demanding something every second to take my attention away from you, wouldn't she?"

Martha pursed her lips then replied: "Yes. Yes, she would! She's never liked me."

"It's not you, personally," Ron suggested with a chuckle, "just anyone with the audacity to steal her baby boy away from the nest." He laughed wickedly, then winced with what looked like sudden pain.

"You alright?" Martha asked, with concern.

"Yeah, fine," Ron said, sounding somewhat strained and breathless, before reaching out for a kitchen chair, pulling it out and sitting down. He closed his eyes for a moment.

"Really? Ron? You don't look well," Martha said, bending to peer at his face closely.

Ron opened his eyes and flashed her a forced smile. "I'm absolutely fine," he said. "It's passed, whatever it was. I just felt a bit funny for a minute, that's all."

"What do you mean, that's all?" Martha exclaimed. "That's not normal. You should maybe go for a check-up."

"Yeah, I'll look into it," Ron replied weakly and pulled his phone out of his pocket to avert his attention to browsing social media. "Ooh, Greg has messaged me. Golf tomorrow, don't mind if I do."

Martha frowned and kissed him on the forehead. "I mean it," she said curtly. "Get checked out."

She slid the baking tray, loaded with glossy dark brown paste, onto the middle shelf of the oven and turned up the music to bring some power to her cleaning up operation. With her hands on her hips, she examined the mess before making a decision and starting by running hot water in the basin. It was time for some more out of time singing, complete with the odd wrong word thrown in as she washed up. Ron couldn't bear to hear Marvin Gaye's efforts so badly interpreted by his wife and took off for a shower, shaking his head and laughing as he left.

CHAPTER 15 – LISA

Straddling her paddleboard, legs either side, as she did every time she went out on the water, Lisa was attempting to be mindful and clear her head.

The words "stupid bitch" were circling around and around in her conscience, stopping her from letting go. *I can't believe she called me that. I should have said to her that she has no idea how hard it's been over the past year. That selfish little girl has no idea what it's like to lose both parents at once. If I had just driven them to the airport like they asked maybe they'd still be here. Anyway… I'd never have spoken to my mum like that. Who the hell does she think she is? Yes, it must be boring for a teenager here. Yes, she's far away from her dad now so that asshole has the perfect excuse to hardly see her, but what can I do about it? He hardly pulled his weight when she lived just one bus ride away from him. It's not going to make any difference. But, no, Clara thinks I'm a demon who's snatched her away from her father, her friends, her beloved shops. For God's sake. Can't she see I was cracking up, needing something else…some quiet place? She'll never understand.*

Lisa's whole body was stiff. She suddenly noticed her white knuckles as her hands clutched the paddle tightly. Instead of breathing and listening to the water making its percussion soundtrack with a smile, today she was frowning at the vast expanse of water. It was a beautiful day with only light peaks of waves and a smattering of clouds concealing the sun. Not warm, not cold.

I should be enjoying this, she thought. *I'm even mad at*

the seals over there just staring at me like I owe them some entertainment. They have it easy. I doubt their pups call them bitches and blame them for every little upset in their self-centred world. I came out here to unwind and put these thoughts away...so...go away!

Her grasp suddenly eased and her shoulders dropped as she felt a pang of pity for her frustrated daughter. She glanced towards the village, almost begging it to offer some excitement, some fun for her girl. *Come on Brogie Bay, show up and give Clara some decent friends. I don't even care if I catch her drinking in the park... in fact, I want to catch her drinking in the park because at least then she'd be having a laugh, being a normal teen, rebelling against me in a way I can understand and that shows she's on the right track.*

Lisa glanced at her watch, a fancy waterproof gadget that told her all the stats she needed about weather, tides, times, distances, heartrate. She'd only been out on the water for fifteen minutes but she decided to call it a day and turn back to land. She was too uptight to even let the sea calm her down. A glass of deep, sexy red in her conservatory, surrounded by decadent plants and lamps, like an upmarket hotel lounge – that's what she needed. That would do the job.

She put her shoulders and core into paddling back towards the concrete slip where she'd set off from and became aware of shrieks and laughter flowing their way across the water surface from that direction. She could make out the heads and shoulders of four people in the calm water at the bottom of the slip. Swimmers. She gasped. *It must be outrageously cold at this time of year. It's only May. The water's still pretty damn cold. Crikey.*

As her board sailed closer towards the group, she could make out the faces of four women. "Hi ladies. Please excuse me as I try not to run anyone over with this board," she called out with a laugh.

Four huge grins beamed at her. "You can give us a lift on that if you like. I fancy going along the coast to Findhoun for a cocktail!"

Lisa laughed and jokingly replied: "You're on." She then added: "What's it like? The water? You must be freezing."

One of the women, sporting a bright pink swim cap, said: "Yep, bloody freezing. But also amazing. My body has stopped feeling sore and now it's just buzzing."

"Sore? Wow," Lisa responded with a grimace.

"You can pop your board on the slip and join us if you fancy," said another swimmer with curly auburn hair and a warm smile. "We're trying to build up our group numbers so we'll have plenty buddies to do this with."

Lisa paused in thought. "Really? What's the group?"

"Brogie Bay Dookers," they all responded with almost perfect time, but enough overlaps and delays to edge away from creepy and robotic. Laughter followed at the near-unison reply.

"Cool," said Lisa, brightening up and no longer feeling the weight of her argument pulling her down like there was concrete inside her wetsuit. She hopped off her board into knee-height water and pushed it up onto the first part of concrete. She turned and pondered the invitation, her heart pounding with the rush of uncertainty and excitement. She wanted to, but at the same time, was she prepared to be cold and wet? She did have a swimsuit on under the wet suit, but everything above the knee was warm and dry at this stage.

"Come on in," beckoned one swimmer with a wry smile. "Stay in your wetsuit if you want, it's fine. No judgement here."

Lisa waded in, keeping her neoprene protective layer on, but keen to be involved in the session. The women widened their circle and said their names – Brydie, Kim and Martha – reassuring Lisa that they were genuinely opening up to her.

"And over there, that's Ray," said Kim. "She's giving thanks to the universe...or the sea...I think...and then she'll come back to the group."

Lisa looked over at the woman who was a picture of serenity, her eyes fixed on the horizon, hands clasped together under her chin as if in prayer, her mouth in motion as she whispered words to the water with a soft expression of contentment on her delicate face. Her claret-red hair was piled up on her head in a messy bun and pale blue flowers were clipped into the bun, which Lisa thought gave her the essence of a sea fairy or some sort of mythical creature.

"I'm Lisa," she offered. "I moved here from Glasgow... not long ago. It's nice to meet some people, to be honest."

"Oh wow," Kim commented. "What brought you up here?"

Lisa cautiously told them the tale of needing to find somewhere quiet to live with her family, leaving out a few details, such as family feuds, an ex-husband, a new wife, trauma and money. She needed to know these dookers a lot better before explaining her entire saga.

"I'm that wanker that lives up on the hill," she said with an enthusiastic eye roll.

"What do you mean, wanker?" Martha asked in confusion. "What have you done to deserve that title?"

Lisa laughed, "Oh, it's just...I get that it's not taken very well when people move into the village and buy up one of the biggest buildings around. It's practically a stately home," she added sheepishly. "But honestly, it needs *so* much work. It's full of '70s carpets and faded wallpaper. We're doing it up slowly. I'm a teacher so I'm not made of money – it'll take a while."

"That doesn't make you a wanker, sweetie," Martha said, tilting her head to the side.

Lisa sighed. "I've heard people talking," she responded. "I heard someone saying we're lording it up and that incomers stop young people being able to buy property and so on."

Brydie laughed: "Oh my god, don't listen to any of the gossip mafia. Seriously, what young person is going to have the funds to buy a house like that anyway? Get real." She quickly added: "Not you. I wasn't telling *you* to get real. I meant anyone who's going to criticise house buyers can get real. It can be a bit like that in small communities – people like to have their say on every little move. Thing is, they can't handle it when the curtain twitchers turn on *them*. There's always some scandal going on, it's actually really funny."

Kim nodded in agreement. "My neighbour was watching me coming home from Brydie's a bit drunk one night, arms folded, looking all prudish. Then the next day she and her husband were yelling at each other so badly I had to take the kids in from the garden and shut all the windows and blast music to drown out the swearing. It was so funny when she caught my eye taking her washing in later that day. She was mortified. No-one's perfect, so no-one should judge. Anyway, what are they judging you for? Doing well for yourself?"

"I guess so," Lisa answered meekly.

"So, do you have family up there?" Martha probed. "Hubby? Kids?"

"A wife," Lisa replied. "And a daughter."

Martha smiled. "Would they come swimming too?"

Lisa felt lighter. She'd only come out recently, when she met Heather. It was relatively new to her to be open and proud. After being married to Owen – a tall, conventionally good-looking policeman - for eight years, it had come as a shock to everyone in her world. Her in-laws were outraged at their perfect son and brother being discarded so she could go in a completely new direction. Her friends were split – some were delighted she was finally owning up to her real self and taking bold steps to be happy and others were catty behind her back, taking pleasure in watching the marital home dissolve and Lisa having to start again in a small rental flat. She quickly learned who was on her team and who needed to be cut off. Some friends, she realised, were only happy to be seen with her when she was riding high on mainstream 'success' with a husband, a kid, a nice detached house and no drama. Lisa was the farthest one could be from a drama queen. All she wanted was to live what felt right.

When Heather visited school as a nurse to deliver flu nasal sprays, they hit it off straight away. There were unbelievable sparks of excitement when they spoke, like she'd never experienced before. They swapped numbers under the guise of attending a pilates class together – which they did indeed do… but pilates soon evolved into drinks nights…which then melted into declarations of lust and love and the realisation that Lisa had been hiding her true desires for years. She'd gone down the path of what she thought she had to do in life to make her parents proud.

The day she came out to her mum and dad was one that would never fade in Lisa's emotionally-scarred memory.

Her mum was sobbing about what her friends would say and with "worry". Lisa always remembers saying: "Why on earth would you be worrying about your daughter finding happiness? True happiness? I've never been so alive. Everything makes sense now. This is who I am. Clara will be absolutely fine, she still has two parents who love her and I'll do right by her. Heather loves her, they get on great."

Those words did little to comfort her mother who, in all honesty, rather enjoyed something to fret over. The statement about two loving parents also ended up throwing a little egg on Lisa's face, as that could hardly be evidenced now, two years down the line, when contacting Owen was a bit like ringing a busy call-centre where it would take a caller several hours, lorries full of patience, the promise of their soul and a million pounds to actually be connected to the right person, voice to voice, human to human. At least that's what it felt like to Lisa. And, indeed, to fifteen-year-old Clara, who could never get hold of her dad. Some promises, Lisa simply couldn't keep, through no fault of her own. And two loving parents was one of them.

Before moving up north, Lisa had grown sick of bumping into friends and having to relive the process of explaining she was no longer with Owen and that the insanely beautiful woman with Turkish heritage, giving her dark chocolate eyes and jet black glossy hair, standing next to her in whichever supermarket or coffee shop they were in was her new partner. She regularly recognised the flicker of shock across their faces and it was exhausting. Lisa hated being hot gossip. She didn't follow a bold path for attention. The spotlight was not a place in which she wanted to shine.

It was refreshing to meet brand new people in the sea, who had no history of Lisa whatsoever, who could accept her new life happily and warmly.

Kim chipped in: "Yeah, the more the merrier. Does your wife paddleboard too?"

Lisa shook her head and laughed. "No. Heather's not very outdoorsy. She'll take a walk on the beach with me, but she's not a fan of getting on, or in, the water. She's happier with a paint brush in her hand doing up bits of our house. In fact, that's what she's doing right now. The old servants' room. She's turning it into a hangout for my daughter, so she can hopefully invite friends over."

"That's awesome," Kim said with a nod of approval.

Lisa flipped onto her back, letting the buoyancy of the wetsuit allow her to float in a starfish shape, glad she had embraced the invitation to meet some new, potential, friends. She was also enjoying the chance to be *in* the water instead of on it. It was a whole different feeling being engulfed by its enormity rather than sitting on top of it.

"Do you think you'll join us again?" Brydie asked as they began to wade back to the slipway. Brydie was patting her thighs, which had gone a deep pinky-red shade from contact with the severe cold water. "Lobster thighs," she said, laughing and pointing to the rosy hue.

Lisa laughed. "Yes. Definitely. And I might even brave it to get myself some lobster thighs of my own without this suit."

"Do it!" Kim encouraged pumping the air with her fist. She then added: "Can someone check there's no seaweed in my bum? Honestly. My cheeks have gone so numb they feel weird…like there's something stuck in there."

Brydie let out a huge chuckle and replied: "Yeah, there's

a whole bush of seaweed sticking out of your cozzie. Either that or you badly need to shave."

Kim laughed and shot her friend a faux evil eye. "Seriously though, is there anything there?"

"No," Brydie responded still laughing. She then turned to Lisa and said: "That's another symptom of cold water swimming you should know about – numb body parts. My butt's never been an issue for me, but each to their own. It's always my bingo wings that take hours to warm up," she added, patting the underside of her upper arms.

Lisa grinned. "Good to know, thanks."

Lisa sighed to see the paddleboard and kit that still needed deflated and packed away. She noticed the bathers were changed and sipping hot drinks within minutes. It looked way more appealing than her long process. This could be the way forward.

CHAPTER 16 – BRYDIE

"**H**elp! Brydie! Help!"

Doug's exasperated words rushed through the hallway to the bedroom where they punched Brydie in the face, waking her up abruptly. She sat up immediately, wild hair whipping around her head like a storm cloud.

"What's wrong?" she called out, croakily, forcing her eyes and voice box to kick into action as she attempted to gain balance in the upright world beyond her bed. She squinted at the clock. Four in the morning.

She padded down the hall to find Doug in the doorway of Millie's bedroom with his hands cupped in front of him. They were formed in a bowl shape full of orange liquid. Brydie recognised the smell. She looked into Doug's panicked eyes.

"What do I do with it?" he said, sounding as though he was about to cry.

"What do you mean, 'what do I do with it'? Go to the bathroom and empty your hands," she replied in disbelief.

As Doug left the room the enormity of the problem became clear as she caught sight of her stepdaughter surrounded by a pool of sick. It was even all over the brand new forget-me-not blue rug. She sighed.

"At least I caught some of it in my hands!" Doug cried from the bathroom desperately.

"Oh Millie," she gushed, trying to tiptoe around the enormous orange puddle to get to her stepdaughter. "You look terrible." She winced at the sight of Millie looking like the child from The Exorcist after her projectile vomit display – as white as a ghost with glazed eyes. She was expecting to be told her mother sucked cocks in hell at any moment. She could almost laugh at the state of her family. Doug was now shifting from left foot to right foot in the bedroom doorway, shrugging and asking: "Shall I get towels? Kitchen roll? Erm....the vacuum?"

"Towels first," Brydie ordered. "From the dirty laundry basket – *not* clean ones. Then we'll do hot soapy water and a cloth."

She turned to Millie. "It'll be Ok." She glanced down at the £200 rug in all its sticky, glossy, orange-tinted glory – with chunks of tomato and red pepper skin – and said with absolutely no conviction: "I'm sure it won't stain."

After the sour stench had calmed down ever so slightly and the washing machine was whizzing with the aftermath of illness, Doug and Brydie sat at the breakfast bar with hot tea.

Doug sighed. "I should really get back to bed. I've got a whole afternoon of meetings online. I'm going to be like a zombie."

Brydie nodded, her head full of energy in post-crisis mode. "My sea swim later today will clear *my* head."

Doug paused his mug just before it reached his mouth. "But.... You'll be at home won't you...with Millie? She can't go to school."

Brydie's face instantly creased, giving away her disappointment. "But I've promised the others I'd meet them at eleven. I sort of feel responsible for the group, seeing as I started it."

Doug tilted his head. "Are you for real? It's not like it's a job. You don't *have* to go dooking practically every day."

"I don't go every day," Brydie snapped. "Maybe three times a week."

"Whatever," he said shaking his head. "You'll have to cancel this one though, surely. Or I'm sure they'll manage without you. We can't leave Millie on her own."

"But you'll be here," Brydie said, thrusting her hand out in gesture towards her husband.

"Working," he nodded. "I can't just say, 'Oh excuse me, Martin and all you guests from our new partner firm, I just have to go and mop up some sick and feed the invalid.'"

The couple sat in silence for a moment.

"I guess I'll give it a miss today then," Brydie muttered grudgingly. "You know it's not that I don't *want* to help," she added, softening. "I'm always doing things for the kids. You know I care. It's just...the group has been my outlet. It's making me feel like....like I have a purpose."

Doug's face remained straight. "I love that you have the group. Honestly, I do. But...I think you're letting it distract you from looking for work. Like it's your excuse not to have time for a job."

Brydie's mouth dropped open. "Doug. I'm *trying*. You know I am." She thumped her mug down on the counter and slumped to the living room. There was no way she was getting back in bed, not if *he* would be joining her. The truth was, he'd hit a nerve. She hadn't been looking for jobs. She was scared. She didn't want to feel those inadequate, trapped-for-life feelings any more of having jobs she hated or jobs she couldn't succeed in.

After an hour of watching TV, she drifted off to sleep on the sofa.

Hours later, when she awoke, Doug was tapping away furiously on his computer keyboard in his office and

Millie was fast asleep in bed. Her bedsheets remained unsoiled, thank goodness.

Brydie sighed and made herself a coffee. She pulled out her crafting basket and shook a plastic tub full of glass beads, holding it up to examine the varying shades of green and blue. She had an idea – something that would cheer her up and she pulled a tray into the glare of the overhead light at the breakfast bar and began folding and bending wire, adorned with beads, slipping into her own calm, little world.

Doug entered the kitchen sheepishly. "Morning," he said, meekly.

He was holding an empty coffee mug, clearly there for another caffeine infusion after the terrible sleep they'd had.

"Morning," Brydie replied curtly without looking up.

Doug placed his hand on her shoulder and bent to kiss the back of her stooped neck. "Hey, I'm sorry," he said softly. "I didn't mean those things to come out the way they did."

There was a long pause where nothing was said, but Brydie turned her head towards him, finally breaking her concentration on the beaded wire.

"I know you make a lot of effort with the kids," he continued, "and I do appreciate that. It can't be easy being the stepmum. But I can't work full-time and do it all alone."

Brydie placed her project down and swivelled fully on the breakfast bar stool to face him with her whole body, looking up into his gaze as he stood above her.

"I know that," she said with exasperation. "I would never expect you to do it all alone. I knew when I married you that I'd have to step up and help. I *wanted* to."

She hugged into his soft stomach, feeling the warmth of his skin through his shirt.

"Nothing good ever comes out of a tired, 5am talk does it?" Doug said with a laugh.

Brydie let out a light flutter of laughter too. "True," she agreed. "Remember the argument we had over who was loudest in bed…during sex?"

Doug sighed. "Yes, I do. That got way out of hand. We didn't speak for the rest of the day did we?"

Brydie smirked. "I even packed a bag to go and stay at mum's. But then, we *had* sunk a few bottles of wine too, so I blame booze as well as tiredness."

"Anyway," Doug interjected. "Thank you for helping me in the night, well actually, for taking over and sorting it all. And if you want to go for that swim, I'm sure I could ask someone to cover for me, or postpone a meeting."

Brydie shook her head with a smile. "No, absolutely not. You were right. I'm not obligated to go to every single swim. They understood when I messaged the group. It's just family life, isn't it? I should never have even thought of going when we've got an ill dude."

With a simple forehead kiss, Doug said everything he needed to say in gratitude and love for his wife before he refilled his coffee then went back to his office down the hall.

Millie appeared in the doorway, stiff, white with sticky hair from sick. "I'm hungry," she croaked.

"Oh, I didn't expect you to be up," Brydie said in shock. "Being hungry is a good sign. Let's try something really small to begin with in case you can't keep it down. I've made that mistake many times before. I once ate a massive slice of chocolate cake thinking I was cured of my stomach bug. You do not want to see the colour of what came back up when I hurled."

Millie chuckled weakly. "Can I sit in here to have it? I don't want to stay in my room all day."

"Ok," Brydie agreed, running to grab a blanket from the hall cupboard to put round her shoulders. "Sit here and I'll get you some crackers and spread."

Millie examined the beads and wire on the counter. "Whatcha making?" she asked.

Brydie grinned and picked one up to point out a fin and a nose. "I'm making dolphin brooches for the ladies in my swim group. We wanted some kind of...badge of honour... to show we're a gang."

"That's so cool," Millie enthused, as much as was possible in her weak state.

"Thanks," Brydie replied with a satisfied smile. "I think they'll love it. We can pin them on our big changing robes... you know, those massive jackets you see us in."

When evening rolled in and Doug was watching TV on the sofa, sandwiched between two kids – one perfectly well, one still pale and serious from her spew trauma – Brydie decided to pop over to Kim's to give her the first completed dolphin brooch. She popped it into a tiny organza drawstring bag to make it even more special and stepped out into the cool, dusk air.

As she got to the corner she saw Kim's door open and stopped walking in surprise as she saw Rick step out. He turned back to face the doorway and leaned inward. Kim's arms wrapped around his neck, clearly pulling him in for a kiss, though their faces were concealed by the door frame.

"What the actual..?" Brydie whispered to herself.

She was standing just a few houses away from Kim's, clutching the little drawstring bag, unsure what to do.

Should she just turn around and go home? Kim stepped out and caught sight of Brydie and awkwardly tucked her hair behind her ear and rushed a final good bye to Rick, gesturing him to go.

She turned to face her friend who was close enough to hear her say nervously: "Hey Brydie, fancy seeing you here."

Brydie marched onwards, towards Kim, still in shock but suddenly on a mission. "What the hell was that?" she asked, pointing to Rick's car as it drove off down the road.

Kim looked flustered as she checked her neighbours' windows for audience members. The couple at number thirty-four quickly retreated from their wide-eyed stance at the glass, knowing they'd been caught.

Kim sighed and ushered her friend inside.

"I know," Kim said, burying her head in her hands to hide her face. "It doesn't look good, after everything I've said about him." She let out a groan. "It's alright for you, with your cosy little set-up. I'm here all on my own. Rick reached out. I have a chance at getting a family unit back," she said, a touch of desperation in her tone.

"What do you mean, my cosy little set-up?" Brydie quizzed, offering just a hint of snappiness. She continued: "I've been nursing a sick kid all day, who's not even mine. I don't have my own kids. I can't have them. My life isn't as perfect as you make it out to be."

"At least you have someone paying all the bills," Kim snapped. "I'm struggling here. If Rick can step back in and help it would make all the difference. You have no idea!"

Brydie's mouth flapped open and shut, as she fumbled for her next retort. "So you'd rather go back with someone you can't stand and who let you down numerous times just to have his wallet in the house?"

Kim smarted and pursed her lips. "It's not just his wallet. There a *whole history* between us. You never saw us as a couple. We were amazing at one point. Who's to say we can't get that back? It's no-one's business anyway. I'm sick of being judged."

"Who's judging? I don't judge you," Brydie cried out desperately. "All the nights I've listened to you going on and on about him while we get drunk and I have never once complained or said anything judgemental? Have I?"

"You did it just now!" Kim shouted.

Brydie's face twitched in shock. She grabbed the front door handle and swung it open wide before exiting in the most dramatic style she'd ever pulled off, not even stopping to look back or say bye. She wanted to take a bow for the audience at number thirty-four.

As she strode down the street, her heart pounded in her chest, as anger coursed through her body. It was only when she looked down at the little bag in her hand that tears began to swell. She tucked the brooch into her jacket pocket, took some deep breaths, wiped her eyes with her sleeve and went into her 'cosy, little set-up'.

CHAPTER 17 – MIKE

It was the first of June and a bright, sunny one at that. Mike leant on his balcony railing, sipping coffee – a latte from his fancy new coffee machine. He was all about enjoying the little things in life these days. Why should he drink instant coffee when he could create a café-quality cuppa at home? He was on a mission to be more kind to himself, to use his money for comfort and treats. Afterall, he worked long hours, he deserved it. Right?

There were only a few, misty clouds in the bright blue sky. It was heaven right there in northern Scotland. The sea was at ease, like it was on board with Mike's wishes for a smooth day.

He pondered what to do with these precious hours of freedom. He could walk around the village, but then, wouldn't that be a busman's holiday, as they say? He did that every day at work.

He could drive to the large town nearby...but what for? Shopping? The thought of browsing the many bland chain stores offering the same generic 'bargain' products across the whole of the UK made him shudder. His mates from work would be spending time with their other halves, undoubtedly.

He heard laughter to his left over by the slipway and turned to focus on a group of people. He could just make out the shapes of people in huge coats putting down large bags on the ledge of the sea wall and hugging. His interest was piqued. It was clearly the swim group.

He bit his lower lip in wonder. Should he? Could he? He had found his wetsuit tucked in the back of the wardrobe the day he got home from coffee at Ray's. She had *almost* persuaded him to join the group.

I need something to do, but I'd be the only man, he thought. *I'd probably ruin the essence of the group.*

He frowned. *But I have been invited to join. It's not like I'd be turning up randomly.*

His stomach flipped with nerves. He carried his coffee through to the bedroom and opened the wardrobe door, staring at the red and black wetsuit that hung, ready for action, on the rail. The smell of it alone brought back memories to the only time he'd ever used it so far. His friend from work took him out on a motorboat. He wore the wetsuit thinking he might jump off the boat into the depths and get a thrill from nature. Of course, when the time arrived and they cut the engine to enjoy some peace as the boat bobbed up and down gently, Mike bottled it. He stared down into the dark blue water, knowing the bottom was a whole journey down. So much water. He froze in fear. He opted to enjoy a beer on dry deck instead. But he'll never forget his friend's amused expression and the constant teasing all the way back about 'wetsuit boy' and various scenarios including: "Ha, I bet Mike thinks you need a wetsuit for jumping in puddles" and "Oh, looks like it's going to spit rain later, better keep your wetsuit on, Mike", and "do you wear it in the shower, mate?".

Mike laughed those quips off, raising his beer bottle in faux appreciation of the punchlines, but it had given him a bit of a complex about suiting up again.

He wasn't keen on feeling the sharp sting of the North Sea on his bare skin, however, and he'd been reading up on wild swimming ever since seeing the women in the bay enjoying it. Turned out it was more common to wear a wetsuit than not. He concluded that the Brogie Bay Dookers were hardy souls and he would have to build up to it.

A moment of courage slapped him into action. He tugged the wetsuit off its hanger and thrust it, along with a towel into an old holdall.

He had the boots and gloves to match the suit – Mike was, after all, always fully prepared and researched equipment long before buying it. He had all the gear...and some of the fear.

He lugged the holdall down the communal stairwell, and out into the sunshine, nerves dancing in his stomach the whole time.

He could see the swimmers bobbing up and down in the distance. Faint laughter bounced off the walls in the space between the bay and the harbour, which made Mike smile. This is the kind of activity he wanted for his day off – nature, happy people, new experiences.

He got to the top of the slipway and dumped his bag down with a satisfied thud. His grin turned to a look of uncertainty as the Dookers all started to make their way in his direction.

"Hi," one shouted to him, giving him a wave.

Then Ray spotted him and called out: "Hello Mike! We're just finishing up. It's cold today, despite the sun. Ten minutes is plenty today."

The three women were now traipsing up the concrete slope, water dripping off their chilled-pink skin.

Ray looked down at his bag. "Were you coming in?" she asked in surprise.

He hesitated and stuttered: "No, nah, I was

just....passing. On my way to, er, somewhere."

Ray gave a knowing smile. "That's a shame. You should join the online page so you can see what times are posted for the group to meet. It's stopped me having to run after everyone at the last minute shouting 'wait for me'."

He let out a forced laugh. "Ok, yeah, I might," he said, picking up his bag. "Anyway, nice to see you all. Have a great day."

He turned on his heel and began walking quickly towards home.

"Mike!" Ray called after him.

He turned back hesitantly and forced a smile to conceal his embarrassment at pretending not to have swimming gear in the bag. "Yeah?"

She was wrapped in a huge stripey towel now, patting her torso dry and walking towards him, away from the group.

"I thought you were on your way to somewhere," she quizzed, nodding towards his flat where he had been heading.

"Oh, I meant, on my way *back* from somewhere," he replied, clearly flustered.

Ray smiled and shook her head, saying: "Doesn't matter. I wanted to ask you something."

Mike stayed silent, a look of fear in his eyes.

"Would you like to come to mine for dinner?" she asked with an assured smile. "We get on well, don't we? It would be nice to have some company... a couple of drinks."

Mike swallowed hard, clearly running a thousand thoughts all at once. Ray's eyebrows raised expectantly while she awaited the answer.

"Yes," he delivered boldly. "Yes. That would be really nice. When?"

"Tonight?" Ray suggested shrugging.

Mike's heart raced and before he could spend too long freaking out and thinking of reasons to put off action, like he usually did, a part of his brain saw sense and jumped in there to force out the word "yes".

"It's a date," Ray said, her eyes sparkling on the word date. "Just pop over about seven. I'll make my best risotto."

Mike nodded, unable to say very much.

He gave a shy wave and turned back towards the former fish warehouse that was his home. A huge grin spread across his lips as soon as his back was to Ray and he no longer had to play down his giddy excitement at being asked to have dinner with the most intriguing, most glamorous, forthcoming woman he'd ever met.

CHAPTER 18 – LISA

"**W**hat have I forgotten?" Lisa asked herself as she stood in the kitchen, triple-checking her large shopping bag full of swim gear.

Heather breezed into the room, still in pyjamas. "What, babe?"

"Oh nothing. I just feel like I don't have enough stuff packed. Towel, warm socks, flask, gloves and surf boots… it's all there, it just seems light."

Heather turned to her with an empty coffee mug in one hand and the other hand on her hip. "It must be because you're used to lugging that massive board down to the beach," she said flatly. "You normally have a tonne of shit with you. If you're not even bringing a wetsuit, then of course it's going to feel light."

Lisa smiled. "True. This is so much easier."

Heather giggled. "Famous last words. I want to hear you say that when you're neck deep in the freezing sea with *bare skin*."

Lisa grimaced. "I am a bit nervous. But if those other people can do it and look so…happy…then I can too." She gave an assertive nod, gathered up her things, gave Heather a kiss on the cheek and left the room.

Clara was coming down the stairs, her grey hood pulled up and as far forward as it would go to partially hide her face. It was a truly morose scene – the dark wooden staircase, which creaked in various eerie tones when anyone descended, peeling, faded wallpaper, ancient tarnished brass light fittings and a moody teen.

"Morning, Bara," Lisa said affectionately, unable to stop using the nickname they'd used since toddler days.

Clara rolled her eyes and continued to the bottom of the stairs, creating the final few musical creaks of the soundtrack, and past her mother without a word.

Lisa turned and threw a sarcastic declaration towards her daughter: "Well, top of the morning to you too!" She sighed and continued to the front door, pausing in the boot room with its ornately tiled floor to slip on her trainers.

She pulled the enormous heavy black-painted door open and stepped out into the cool air.

She still couldn't believe, whenever she stood on the stone steps at the entrance to the grand nineteenth century Baronial-style house, that it was theirs. She leant against the stone entrance porch wall and took in the view all the way down the hill to the village with its granite stone cottages, surrounded by blue ocean which stretched on for miles to the mountains of the northern Highlands way off in the distance. It was like something you would make up. An idyllic dream. She took in the sight for a moment, consciously slowing down her breathing and attempting to shun the negative feelings from her hallway encounter.

She glanced to her left at the flaking white paint on the bay window and shuddered. There was so much work to be done to fix up this crumbling mansion. Vegetation was growing up the exterior walls, which Lisa thought looked devastatingly romantic, but estate agents had warned her to "sort that out" immediately or risk extreme damp. She really had bitten off more than she could chew. But the view was exceptional and the large rooms, laden with original features were expectant with potential – if only she had the money. Above all, the house had a tower, complete with cone-shaped roof, like in every fairy-tale castle Lisa had drawn pictures of as a child. She was sold on the place the minute she saw it. The peace and quiet was another attraction to this glorious site by the sea. Her parents had done well in buying and selling properties in their early married life, meaning they had a huge nest egg to pass on to Lisa. She may as well live to her fullest with it – do them proud by doing this place up as a showpiece for all their hard work. The problem was, most of the inheritance money went on actually buying the place. The fifty grand that was left after the keys were in her palm had already mostly been all used up on jobs like weather-proofing the patchy roof tiles, removing awful carpets and paying someone to restore wooden floors and tiles in some of the rooms and putting in a functioning kitchen to replace the hideous 1960s units some previous owner had been so evil as to install. All that was left now was Lisa's teacher wage and Heather's nursing pay. They were using every last penny and Lisa feared the home makeover would be long enough to rival the century-long paint job of Edinburgh's Forth Rail Bridge.

She sighed at the virtual 'to do' list which was now racking up in her mind at the sight of her sprawling house and turned her back on it to get into the car – a modest Fiat, quite the juxtaposition next the grandeur of the house.

A few minutes later, Lisa was parking at the harbour, flutters of anxiety swishing in her core at the thought of being with new people as well as doing something brand new in the cold ocean.

She joined the flurry of changing robes, bags and boots

at the top of the slipway.

"Hi," she said nervously.

Martha turned to greet her. "You came! Fantastic."

"Yep," Lisa nodded. "And no wetsuit."

Brydie gave her two thumbs up and said "Excellent" with an excited grin.

Ray clasped her hands together in prayer formation and beamed a warm smile in Lisa's direction as if to say 'welcome'.

"I know it's June, but isn't this still a cold time of the year for the sea?" Lisa asked with hesitance.

Brydie smiled. "Well, yes. The water won't really warm up until late summer, about September. And even then, we're in northern Scotland, so it's never going to get really comfortable." She pulled a jokingly fearful expression.

Lisa stroked her forehead in thought as she examined the still water. "Well, it *looks* divine," she said with a laugh. "No turning back now."

She pulled off her hoodie to reveal a black swimsuit underneath and began pulling on her protective boots.

When the group were all ready and gave each other the nod of approval, they started walking down the slip, giggling and chattering as they stepped.

Lisa's mind was churning over several thoughts at once, some telling her to go for it, others telling her it's OK to back out. She was already chilly from the ten degree Celsius air temperature. If she was sprouting goosebumps on her arms and legs already, that surely meant she wouldn't have the resilience for chilly water.

Being stubborn and proud, she stepped in sync with the others and kept going. Her calves hit the cool water, sending a shock through her body. Yet more stepping. Her thighs were submerged now and her breathing grew quicker and deeper. Martha let out a shriek as her nether region hit the chill and the others laughed before they, too, were gasping and shouting that the water was now above their 'temperature gauges'.

Before Lisa could really work out what they meant, the next step she took brought the water up to her waist level and she felt the blast of cold to her private parts and laughed at the realisation of what they group meant by 'temperature gauge' – one of the most sensitive parts of one's anatomy.

Brydie turned to Lisa. "You alright?" she asked affectionately.

Lisa nodded, taking deep breaths. She decided to splash her arms with sea water to help them adjust before it would be time to submerge and swim. "Argh, holy crap that's cold!" she shouted with laughter as sprinkles of pain danced on her body.

"Three, two, one...in!" Martha called out and with that, the three women up ahead all pointed their hands out in arrow-shapes and dove gently forward, floating into a swim position and submerging their shoulders. It was a beautiful sight watching them surrender to floating in synchronicity. Lisa grinned.

"OK, count me down then," she called after them.

The women up ahead turned and counted her down with rapturous enthusiasm, making Lisa feel pumped and revitalised. "Three, two, one...in!" And with that, Lisa's whole body became buzzed and alert as she glided forward in gloriously clear water. She could see a crab below, scuttling towards the safety of the nearest seaweed bloom.

She allowed herself to float, calmly for a minute, soaking in the sights of pebbles and shells under her body.

"I love a calm day like this," Brydie said with a serene smile. "It's like a swimming pool today...just calm."

Ray tilted her face up to the sky, eyes closed and declared: "Thank you universe."

After a few minutes of letting their bodies settle into the activity, the women formed a circle and began chatting.

"Wow, I don't feel the stinging feeling anymore," Lisa said in wonder.

"It's amazing isn't it?" Martha enthused. "After the initial shock, you just feel lovely. I never thought I'd be doing this. I get sore hips and backpain and, honestly, when I'm here and for a few hours afterwards it's like – what pain? It's magical."

"It's a shame Kim couldn't make it," Ray said, looking at Brydie.

Brydie's expression changed from serene to troubled as a frown creased the space between her eyebrows. She shrugged. "Yeah. She's busy today."

"What's she up to?" Martha asked innocently.

"I dunno," Brydie commented, looking off into the distance. "Something with the kids probably."

Ray and Martha exchanged quick glances of concern.

"Oh well," Martha said with forced cheeriness. "Maybe she'll join us next time. It's a busy life being a mum. In fact, it's a busy life being a daughter. I'm heading to my parents' after this. They're not doing so well. Dad's fully dottled and mum's on her way there I think."

"Oh, that's stressful for you," Ray offered, with a depth of sincerity. "I never had to deal with that with my parents because we never spoke. I didn't even know they were dead until the lawyer found me. We just never had that closeness. I'm a solo bird. And there'll be no-one to check in on me when I'm dottled." She laughed at that final thought. "You'll just see me wandering the village talking to myself."

"So, no difference then," Martha teased with a laugh.

Ray let out a snort of laughter. "Cheeky bitch." She splashed salty water towards her new friend. "You're right though, no-one will be able to tell when I've lost the plot."

Lisa stayed silent. She wanted to open up about losing both her parents. She wanted to ask for reassurance that it's OK to go on enjoying life after grief but it felt more like a day to observe and get familiarised than bare her soul. She noticed her arms tingling and commented on this to the others.

"Ah, it could be time to get out now," Brydie said decisively. "Always listen to your body. If you go past that lovely point where your body feels fine and you start to notice the cold again then don't hang around. You'll end up with the shakes and that's not fun. I had the shakes last week… for about two hours after I went home. That taught me just to call it quits before you actually want to come out. It's too tempting to stay in chatting, but it's not worth it. Your core temperature is going to keep dropping even when you get out."

Lisa listened to the advice intently, glad she had more experienced people to learn from.

"Dress as quickly as you can and get a hot drink," Brydie added.

The group all began heading for land, discussing their plans for the rest of the day and exchanging words about how great they felt after that blast of adrenaline.

Lisa patted herself dry while Ray sloped off to speak to a guy who'd turned up at the last minute. She heard

Martha whispering: "It's the postie. Do you think he wanted to join us?"

"I think so," Brydie replied. "Poor guy just missed his chance. If he'd been ten minutes earlier he could have come."

Finally in clothing, the group sat on the thick stone wall sipping hot liquids from various flasks.

"I have a surprise," Martha declared, producing a plastic tub full of brownies. Anyone passing would be mistaken for thinking she was handing out bars of gold, there was that much excitement around the tub. The chilly women all gathered up chunks of brownie enthusiastically, feeding their exhilarated bodies with the gooey, sweet treasure.

Except Ray. "I have my own," she said with a grin and pulled out a small piece of cake wrapped in a napkin from her crocheted shoulder bag. She winked at Martha and Martha rolled her eyes in amusement.

Lisa wasn't exactly sure what was going on, but she was too busy devouring the rich, chocolatey treat to care.

Soon after, Ray, gathered up all her belongings, swung her damp towel over her shoulder and said: "Right...I must go darlings. It was fabulous as always, but I have to prepare for... a date!"

The group exploded in intrigue.

"Who's the lucky man?" Martha asked, then added quickly... "or woman?"

Ray just tapped the side of her nose and winked. "That would be telling," she said with a sadistic smile.

"Oh Ray! Come on!" Brydie pleaded with a laugh.

"In time, my dears. In time," Ray responded slyly.

"Well... I'm sure we can guess anyway," Brydie added with raised eyebrows. "We saw you having a little chat with the postie. He seemed a bit flustered."

Ray turned on her heel, gave a giddy wave and fled for her cottage across the green. "Bye bye. I'll fill you in another time... if there's anything worth telling!"

Lisa was highly amused. This was going to be fun. The group was far from boring. Just what she needed.

After saying her good byes, Lisa made her way back up the hill, parking in her driveway, enjoying the familiar sound of tyres on gravel – which was always like ringing out a bell to say "I'm home".

She burst into the house, looking for anyone to share her news with. Clara was on the sofa, eyes fixated on her phone in the sitting room. It always made Lisa feel uneasy to see her modern black leather sofa plonked in an ancient room which demanded a much bigger, more opulent sofa, but it would have to do for now. She shook that thought from her head and proceeded to excitedly tell Clara about the swim.

"I did it! I did cold water swimming, in just skins – that's what they call just a swimsuit apparently," Lisa enthused, barely taking a breath. "It was amazing, I felt..."

"Good for you," Clara grunted before standing up and heading for the door, pushing past her mum to leave.

Lisa stopped mid-sentence. "Hey, no need to be rude," she said with a tinge of frustration. "I'm only trying to tell you about something I've pushed myself to do. Something I'm proud of."

There was no response from Clara, who was now in the kitchen perusing the contents of the open fridge.

"I made some new friends," Lisa continued, moving into the kitchen. "Maybe you could..."

"Big deal," Clara interrupted, slamming the fridge door. "You met some hippies who want to freeze their tits off too. Sounds so much fun." She looked her mother square in the face. "And I know what you were just about to say, that I should make some friends too. Just like you, because you're perfect and everyone loves you. Well, I don't want to make friends with anyone I've met here so far. They all think I'm weird. I'm the weirdo with two mums who lives in the creepy Addams Family house. It looks a right state and everyone thinks it's haunted. My room stinks of old socks too."

Lisa was stunned. "How dare you be so rude? I've tried *so hard* to give you a better quality of life," was all she could think of to say, before her rational brain stepped in and told her to attempt to see things from the teenager's side. "And anyway, who has an issue with you having two mums? Not that Heather is your mum, but anyway... has anyone said anything? Do you want me to talk to the school?"

Clara folded her arms and looked down. "No. No-one has said anything, don't go phoning the school."

Lisa realised, Clara must be using anything in her arsenal to try and get at her. The two mums quip was not really an issue at all. Lisa knew how much Clara liked Heather. It wasn't really about that at all.

"Is there anything you want to talk about?" Lisa asked. "Anything I can help with?"

Clara rolled her eyes. "Classic. Turn it back on me. I'm the problem."

She stormed past her mum, words spilling out of her mouth the whole way. "You don't see it do you mum? You force me to live up here, away from my friends, away from dad, make me stand out as the only one who doesn't live in a normal house like everyone else...you come in boasting about how much fun you're having and if I complain at all, you pull the 'my parents are dead' card as if I'm not allowed to feel anything because you have it worse."

"Wow," Lisa exclaimed in shock. "I never even mentioned granny and grandad. I had no idea you could be so downright nasty."

"Yeah, maybe I should go and live with dad because I'm just a nasty, little loser who's cramping your style," Clara said with venom in every word.

"Good luck with that!" Lisa retorted. "That asshole wouldn't have you. He barely even managed his weekend visits with you! He's not interested!"

Those words stabbed Clara's soul before Lisa's eyes, causing Lisa's stomach to churn. Her face crumpled into sorrow and she moved towards Clara desperately saying: "I'm sorry. I didn't mean it to come out like that."

Clara was already halfway up the creaking stairs, hiding her face. "Fuck off mum. Just fuck off."

Lisa gasped, frozen at the bottom of the stairs. She started to climb after her daughter, but Heather appeared from behind, placing her hands on Lisa's shoulders. "Leave her for a bit," Heather said softly. "Let her cool down before you talk to her. She's hurting."

Lisa turned around and sobbed into Heather's shoulder.

"I'm such a bad mum. I've ruined everything. I didn't think moving up here would cause all this. I thought she'd get a better quality of life." Lisa wiped her eyes with her hoodie sleeve and let out an anguished sob.

"Shhh," Heather soothed as they moved through to the living room. "Just breath."

CHAPTER 19 – RAY

Steam billowed upwards from the hot, bubbly water in the roll-top bath. Ray was sprawled out, enjoying the hot water surrounding her body. It was quite the contrast to the chilly sea water she'd embraced just two hours ago. Her body was finally fully warmed up. Now it was time to prep for wooing Mike.

The open window let birdsong trickle into the room and mingle with the Middle Eastern beats she had playing from an old CD player in the hallway, which was aimed at the open bathroom door. It was calming perfection for Ray.

She lifted a leg out of the bubbles and weighed up her options. To shave or not to shave? That was the question. Ray sat uncomfortably in the middle of this debate. She very rarely shaved. Why should she? If women were intended to be hairless they wouldn't grow hair – that was her gut feeling on the matter. But, as was drummed into her from an early age, if you're starting a potential new relationship you want to present your best self. She sighed.

I don't want to conform to the hairless society. I am who I'm meant to be....however, I get the feeling Mike isn't quite ready to take on this woman in all her yeti glory.

She laughed and thought, *I bet he'd surprise me. There's something about him. Something primal, strong, unshakeable. I could probably come at him with bushy armpits and he'd embrace it. Anyway, it's just a meal. We aren't going to be rolling around in bed together... just yet!*

Still, it's better to be preened and prepared so I feel like a seductress. If I had a penny for all the times I've been caught out in full winter fur when I wasn't expecting romance...

She tutted, already disappointed in herself for conforming to feminine standards and reached over to the end of the bath for her razor to make herself silky smooth.

After getting out, she spent considerable time moisturising head to toe with expensive, handmade cream from an organic farm nearby, knowing that was the very reason her sixty-year-old skin was still supple and glowing.

The following hour was spent choosing which floaty maxi dress of the dozens to wear – a midnight blue one with sequin swirls – drying and curling her crimson hair and adding just enough makeup to enhance her sparkly eyes without looking like she was putting on a stage show. She popped in a blue gem nose stud and squeezed her dainty wrists into a whole collection of spangly bangles picked up on her travels over the years. It gave her a melodic jingle with every flick of the wrist. After examining the finished product in a full-length mirror and giving herself a nod of satisfaction, she made her way to the kitchen to get started on the promised risotto. She pulled the CD player through with her and switched to Ella Fitzgerald – something she could sing to. Singing and a swift glass of merlot settled her nerves, because, as much as Ray was a woman of the world, she was feeling a little uptight and giddy at the thought of spending time with Mike. It had been years since she'd shown any interest in the male species. All the men around Brogie were pleasant enough, but lacking in spice, according to Ray. In more plain words – bloody boring. Mike, on the other hand, intrigued her. He was rugged, yet soft. He lit up with an unusual spark when he listened to her. This threw her off her usually unflappable course. She was, most definitely, flapped.

Risotto successfully made and left in the pan with the lid on for later, Ray sat in the living room, sipping her second glass of merlot. *Slow down girl,* she thought. *If you get too merry before he arrives you'll throw yourself at him and that's never been a wise move, has it? You want this one to marinade slowly.*

Time seemed to slow right down to a painful drag while she waited for Mike to arrive. She plumped cushions, lit incense, lit candles....moved candles....changed her seating position several times. She was restless. She rested her chin in her palm, leaning on the arm of the sofa and felt a bristly, little hair poking out from her chin.

"Argh! Tweezers," she shouted out loud. She ran to the bathroom to locate and eradicate the blighter. She spotted two more – the perils of growing older. With her eyesight not quite what it used to be, she didn't always notice when the hairs were back in chin town until there was a whole gang of them. This called for better lighting. The best spot for plucking was by the living room window with a hand-held magnifying mirror Ray kept in the bottom drawer of the living room drawers. She sat on the windowsill and angled her neck so that the sunlight caught any stray bristles on her skin and illuminated them. She began plucking – it was a bigger job than she anticipated. Mid-concentration, Ray suddenly became aware of movement in her peripheral vision. Blimey! Brenda from next door was waving ecstatically through the glass. Ray, thrust the tweezers and mirror down on the ledge, mortified, and gave a cautious wave and forced smile back. *Can't a woman pluck in peace around here?*

Resigned to the fact that she'd got rid of as many unwanted hairs as possible, she slumped into an armchair and attempted to peruse a coffee table photography book of waterfalls. It would help pass some time. But...it didn't. She was unable to really focus on it.

Finally, there was a self-assured knock on the door. Ray jumped out of her seat, tousled some life into her hair, exhaled forcefully, took a deep breath in and made for the door.

As she opened it, her breath caught in her throat with nerves, or excitement, or both intertwined.

"Good evening," she enthused, a little short of breath.

"Hello," Mike said cheerily, holding up a bottle of sparkling wine. "I didn't know what to get, so I thought... fizz for a glamorous lady."

Ray beamed. "Wonderful. Thanks. Come in and let's get this baby popped."

As she fumbled about in kitchen cupboards she called through to Mike: "I'm so sorry I don't have matching champagne flutes anymore. We'll have to be unmatching."

Mike laughed. It was the last thing on his mind. He let out a breath he hadn't realised he'd been holding. "I don't mind," he said quietly.

Ray reappeared in the living room holding one plain champagne flute and a second flute with gold intricate patterns painted all over it. She grimaced at that glass. "It was actually a present from Richard Branson once. Well, it was part of a set, but it's the last remaining one. Very expensive apparently. I always end up smashing them. I can't keep a set of glasses."

Mike laughed. "How did you know Richard Branson?"

Ray shook her head to dismiss the subject, "Oh that's a story for another time," she teased. "I don't think you're ready for that."

He grinned as she tilted each glass and poured the bubbling golden liquid. They clinked glasses and Ray offered the words: "To new friendships and fun times."

"Perfect," Mike agreed then took a sip. "That first sip is always such a nice treat."

Ray tilted her head back, exposing her long neck. "Oh my gosh yes. I love it. You can't beat a glass of bubbly. You have good taste, kind sir. Take a seat."

Ray pointed to the mustard velvet sofa, giving her guest no choice of where to sit. She sat next to him, leaving a body's width between them out of respect.

"So…" Mike searched for the next piece of conversation with which to pave their way to comfort and ease. "Did you enjoy your swim?"

"Oh yes," Ray gushed. "Honestly, joining that group is giving me a new burst of energy. I really don't know why I wasn't already swimming all the time. The sea has been right there, on my doorstep, the whole time, and I've only just woken up to the rush of plunging in."

"It's getting quite popular now isn't it – the wild swimming scene," Mike commented, adding: "I've seen bits on TV and in the papers about people doing it for their mental health or illnesses."

"Yes, absolutely," Ray agreed. "I think we've reached a point on the planet where we need to reconnect with nature. We've become so technological, so dependent on luxuries and modern living that something has disconnected between humans and nature. And people are seeing that. They want to get back to being more in tune with it. It's what's real. The other stuff is all fabricated. We weren't created to drive fancy cars or watch screens. Anyway, I'm going on a bit now," she finished with a smirk. "I do that, just so you know."

Mike smiled. "It was interesting. And I totally agree."

"You were going to join us today, weren't you?" Ray asked sensitively, clearly aware he had hidden that fact earlier due to embarrassment.

Mike's face reddened slightly and he shifted in his seat before taking a big gulp of fizz and replying: "I did think about it, yes. I had my wetsuit ready and I just thought 'sod it, let's do this' but I got the timing wrong."

"It's exciting that you're up for it," Ray said warmly. "Next time."

"I dunno," Mike said, rubbing his short grey beard. "Won't it be weird if I'm the only man, AND wearing a wetsuit. When I saw all you ladies without wetsuits, I thought 'well, I'm going to look like a right fanny then aren't I?'"

"Nonsense," Ray protested. "Wear whatever the hell you like. They're such a nice bunch, they won't care. And we don't want to keep it to an exclusive female only group. Anyone's welcome. It would be kind of nice to open it up and maybe more guys will start joining if they see you."

Ray glanced at the patterns on Mike's dark green, short-sleeved shirt. "Oh, I didn't realise there were animals hidden in the pattern. Very nice. You're an interesting guy aren't you," she said, raising an eyebrow.

"What do you mean, interesting? That sounds like I have bad taste." He let out a chuckle.

"On the contrary," Ray insisted. "I like a man who wears bold clothing – a man who's not afraid to stand out.

And your arm full of tattoos. That's intriguing," she said, moving a little closer on the sofa to inspect his ink. She ran her fingers along the body of a snake which wound around his forearm and was aware of Mike stiffening up. She glanced up into his eyes with a mischievous smile. He didn't know how to respond. This was all a little quick for physical contact.

Sensing this, Ray shifted further back again on the sofa with a grin. "Don't worry, I'm not going to pounce on you," she said with a glint in her eye. "But I do think you're very handsome."

Mike gulped. "I'm, I'm…not used to such directness," he said with an air of disbelief.

An awkward eight seconds passed by. "I think you're… very beautiful," he finally replied.

Ray held his gaze firmly for a minute, as if sending him subliminal sexual messages that he may as well surrender now because she had a long-term game plan. He could clearly sense this as he nervously tipped the last of his drink down the hatch and clutched the empty glass tightly with both hands.

Ray changed the tone by announcing "Let's eat!" and she left Mike to pour new drinks while she reheated the garlic mushroom risotto. Ray had only used half the normal amount of crushed garlic she would normally use…just in case kissing was on the cards.

"Your candle's gone out," Mike called from the living room.

Ray shouted in reply from the kitchen: "Can you take a new tealight from the top drawer next to the window, please?"

She grated parmesan on top of the steaming hot bowls of rice and then suddenly froze. *Shit. The golden nipple!*

She dashed to the doorway just in time to see Mike standing by the open drawer holding a small golden ornament with utter confusion painted on his face.

"That's... well, it's my golden nipple," Ray said, shrugging, defeated by reality with no other way to explain it.

Mike looked from the nipple in his palm, to Ray, then back to nipple. Eventually he found some words. "I thought it was a candle. I was about to try and light it." He started to laugh sheepishly.

"Easy mistake to make," Ray offered in amusement. "Let me explain...a boyfriend in the '80s – my first love actually, Will – made a cast of my nipple for part of a mixed media artwork. He was an art student at the time, in London."

Mike placed it back in the drawer carefully and nodded to signal he understood, but he had gone pretty quiet.

"It seems weird now, right?" Ray said a bit hesitantly. "I keep thinking I should bin it, but then I think, no. It's part of my history. He was very talented and we were crazy about each other. Well, until he wasn't anymore."

Ray stared at the drawer for a moment. "Anyway, you absolutely do not want to hear about my exes! This is *our* evening. I'll just bring the food."

Ray breezed gently back into the kitchen, a small frown on her forehead. Was she too much for Mike? She had planned on being mysterious and not too zany on this first date. *Typical Ray style*, she thought, *bring out the tales of weirdness to freak him out before you've even served dinner.*

When she entered the living room with the two helpings of hot, creamy risotto, she searched his face for signs of discomfort, but it was hard to tell.

As if sensing this, he reached out for his bowl of food and said reassuringly: "By the way, it was a very nice ornament." He let out a hearty giggle and Ray's concerned expression eased into a rounded smile once more.

As they ate, Ray gave Mike a light grilling and discovered he had been previously married.

"Oh darling, if you get to our age and haven't been married then that's a bit unusual," she reassured.

"Have you been married?" he asked.

Ray practically guffawed and had to concentrate on swallowing her food properly for fear of choking on it due to laughter. "Yes...a few times. My husbands were a bit like cheap glue – none of them stuck."

"Husbands plural? How many?" Mike asked, his eyebrows slightly raised and his fork paused in mid air.

Ray looked up at the ceiling and made facial gestures as if she could see images of them in the air and was physically counting them. "Three times," she finally revealed. "Divorced twice and widowed once."

"Wow. Sorry, that must have been tough."

"Yeah, none of it's easy is it? The dead one would have ended up in divorce anyway. He went off to America and someone told me he had a drugs overdose, but I heard from someone else a few years later that he actually had cardiac arrest on a mechanical bull ride – a bucking broncho thing. Who knows? I prefer the second version. That would be a more fitting way for him to go. He was always riding something!" she added with a wicked laugh.

There was silence, save for the light double bass notes floating through from some soft jazz CD in the kitchen.

Mike opened his mouth. Closed it again, thought for a moment and said: "You really have some tales to tell, don't you?"

"Enough about me," she said, smiling warmly. "Tell me more about you."

They passed some time chatting about life as an incomer to northern Scotland and music tastes. It was very obvious that Mike was finally relaxing into the evening. Ray vowed to herself to only drip feed the odd anecdote from her past every now and then. She didn't want to scare him off. A golden nipple and a back catalogue of failed marriages ending in a potential bull ride death was enough for one date. The story about her love affair with a snake charmer in Morocco could wait... a very long time.

With dinner devoured and plates piled in the kitchen sink, Mike got up to go.

"Thanks so much for dinner," he said, "It was delicious."

Ray, who was just coming back in from the kitchen, stepped close to him, facing him straight on.

"You're not leaving yet, are you? The night is young." A flicker spread across her eyes and Mike gulped.

"I'm really tired," he sighed. "Too many early mornings."

She edged closer, having to tilt her head ever so slightly to maintain eye contact. Neither of them said a word. Ray's body was merely a centimetre away from touching Mike's. He held her gaze intently. The air was charged with potential.

Ray licked her lips, as if in preparation for the off – for the kiss.

Mike stooped his head slightly. Suddenly, his nerves seemed to evaporate and a new heated, focus took over. Ray placed her hand on Mike's chest as his hands slipped around her waist. It was 'game on'.

In utterly terrible timing, the doorbell rang and a mysterious fist banged on the front door several times. It sounded frantic – alarming.

Ray stepped back, heart pounding. "Who on earth could that be?"

She rushed to the door, with Mike following behind her as back-up.

As the door opened, a sorry sight met them. Lisa stood before them, eyes puffy and red in evidence of tears, and a pained expression on her face.

"Hi, sorry, I didn't know where else to go," she explained frantically. "My daughter's gone missing and I remembered you saying at the swim you lived at the house with the windchime by the door."

"Come in, come in," Ray gestured, ushering her new friend inside. "Fill us in and we'll see what we can do to help. We'll find her."

Lisa walked into the living room, spotted the two glasses on the table and heard the jazz notes dancing through from another room. She shook her head. "I'm so sorry. I shouldn't have come. This is your da… you're busy."

"Nonsense," Ray insisted. "Finding your daughter is important. You did the right thing coming to people you know."

Lisa let out a whimper of emotion. "I don't know many people here at all. And Clara doesn't have friends yet, so I can't go knocking on doors." She placed her hand wearily on her forehead as if the racing thoughts of worry were causing her pain.

"When did you last see her?" Mike asked calmly.

"A few hours ago," Lisa replied, regaining focus. "We

had a massive fight after the swim and when I went upstairs to tell her dinner was ready, she was gone. I can't find her. She's not answering her phone and I haven't put on a tracking thing, like other parents do. I thought it was intrusive. How stupid am I? I've driven around the village a few times. I've even been out onto the main roads to see if she's hitch-hiking. Heather's still wandering the streets just now, keeping a lookout." Lisa's face crumpled and she took an enormous, panicked breath in.

Ray placed a hand firmly on her shoulder. "Show us a picture of her and we'll go and look. We know lots of little places the teenagers hang out."

"But how would Clara know where they are if she hasn't got any friends?" Lisa asked, wild fear in her eyes.

"You never know," Ray replied. "She must have heard stuff at school. She's bound to know what goes on. How long have you been here?"

"About seven months."

Mike nodded. "Your daughter probably knows places you don't."

"What if she's already left the area though? Hitch-hiked with some random driver?" Lisa's eyes were framed by the most severely angled frown.

"Phone the police and we'll start looking," Ray reassured her.

CHAPTER 20 –
THE SEARCH

As they left Ray's house, the night air had cooled quite a bit. Mike ran to his for a jacket and arranged to meet Ray by the harbour. There was a good chance Clara might be on the harbour wall anyway, as there were often kids up there, smoking and relishing the danger at such a height from the rocks and seabed on the other side of the wall.

As Ray waited outside Mike's building, she rubbed her arms to keep warm and examined the entire harbour area. Apart from two young lads sitting up high, passing a bottle of beer back and forth in the orange glow of street lamps, there was no other sign of life.

"The bothy?" Ray suggested, shrugging. Mike nodded in agreement.

The bothy was an old ruin of a stone house in the forest which ran alongside the beach. It was definitely known as a gathering place for young people. Gossip queens loved to pass on information in the village shop about what 'so and so' was caught doing in the bothy and therefore "dragged home by the lug".

It would take them a good ten or fifteen minutes to even reach the bothy, but it would be crazy not to check there.

All small talk and flirtatious chat had ceased by this point as they focused on the goal and strode through the dark village streets until they met the entry of the forest.

Ray paused for a moment at the wooden posts flanking either side of the sandy path. She took a deep breath and closed her eyes.

"You alright?" Mike asked gently.

Ray opened her eyes and stared into the woods where it was pitch black at points, with the moon casting a silver glow on parts of tree trunks to give a hint of what lay ahead.

"I'll be fine," she muttered. "I just had a bad experience in a forest once. I was attacked. A bunch of girlfriends and I snuck out of boarding school to smoke in the woods and two guys spotted us and...things got a bit....terrifying. Thankfully, the caretaker had come after us and shot a pistol into the air to scare them off. God knows what would have happened. Poor caretaker got suspended for possessing a gun." Ray sighed. "Anyway, this is the time for me to wear my 'big girl pants' so to speak and just get on with looking for Clara."

"And besides," Mike offered, "you're with me. I won't let anything happen." He smiled at her and produced a torch from his pocket.

"To hell with it," she said with enforced strength as she pushed on into the trees. "I'm not scared of anything anymore. People tend to be scared of *me* these days."

The pair trudged along the sandy path, stepping on bumpy tree roots which had grown up from the depths of soil across the route, causing them to stumble occasionally in the dark. They heard an animal rustling in the trees and stopped, still, to listen.

"Probably a fox," said Ray excitedly, as Mike chased after the sound with the beam of light from his torch just in time to see some bushes dancing wildly as the creature cut through them.

An owl called out way above them.

"I've never been in these woods at night," Mike said, sounding like he was actually enjoying the experience.

"I've done a few solstice meditations with a group at the very edge of the forest where it meets the beach," Ray said, "but I haven't been in this deep at night. Why would I? Although, an old neighbour of mine used to walk his dog here at this time of night. Imagine that. Pitch black walkies. He said his dog preferred it because he always went on attack mode when they met other dog walkers during the day, so this was better."

Eventually, they could make out the bothy clearing up ahead. The sandy ground around it was reflecting moonlight and an orange glow spilled out from the spaces where windows used to be, as a fire blazed inside. They could hear voices – definite teenage voices. There were boys shouting and laughing with that signature teenage tone as their voice boxes fluctuated between booming and deep to squeaky and juvenile. Girls were shrieking and erupting into guttural giggles.

Ray and Mike stopped on the spot, not wanting to go any further. They heard a bottle smashing inside the bothy and a whole array of voices cheering.

When the raucous shouts calmed, Ray grabbed onto Mike's arm for moral support and called out into the clearing: "Clara?"

No response.

"Clara! Are you there?"

A thin girl with long hair and a woollen beanie hat came out of the bothy, silhouetted by moonlight.

"Who's asking?" she said abruptly.

"My name is Ray. I know your mum," Ray responded boldly. "I just want to talk to you."

"Why should I?" came the response.

There was silence while Ray pondered her next sentence. "Why not? What's to lose?"

The girl stood, arms folded, not responding, yet not going back into the bothy either.

"We could sit over there," Ray said, pointing to a huge log that overlooked the sand dunes and down onto the beach.

"Fine. But she's so full of shit, she's probably poisoned you against me," Clara blurted as she walked, grudgingly, over to the log.

"I'll wait back here," Mike whispered. "It'd be better if it was just you."

Ray nodded and walked over to meet the teenager in the moonlight.

They both sat, facing the water, which was reflecting silver light and roaring furiously with foamy waves in the distance. The cool air whipped their hair and Ray wished she also had a hat, like Clara's.

"So, what are you doing out here?" Ray asked, initiating the conversation.

"None of your business," Clara said. "How did you know where I was?"

"Ah, there's not many places for teenagers to go around here," Ray said with a smile. "Us old people know all the hot spots."

Clara's expression remained straight. She had a pretty face with large pale eyes and natural full eyelashes. Even with a scowl on her face she looked rather cute.

"You're going to try to get me to go home, aren't you?" Clara said with a tone of bitterness. "She doesn't even want me there. And she says my dad doesn't want me, so what am I supposed to do?"

"Your mum definitely wants you there," Ray said with a firm tone. "If you could have seen how worried she was when she came to my house, you would know she loves you. She's out of her mind with panic right now."

"Yeah, because she'll get in trouble if anything happens to me," Clara snorted.

"I'm sure there's a lot more to it than that," Ray said softly. "It must have been hard for you moving up here."

There was a pause while Clara digested those words. "Yeah. It's been shit."

"How so?"

"Urgh," Clara sighed in exasperation. "All of it. I'm bored. I'm lonely. I'm worried I'll never see my dad again...or if I do, he won't have anything to say to me because we'll barely know each other anymore."

Ray left those words hanging in the air, leaving space for Clara to continue without being interrupted. "Or worse...I'm scared mum's right and he really doesn't care about me. That's probably more likely."

"I'm sure your mum chose to live here for some very good reasons," Ray finally offered. "She seems like a great person. In fact, if I'm honest, I think she's got giant balls and should be worshipped."

Clara's scowl broke and she let out an involuntary laugh. "What?"

"Well...." Ray continued, "from what I gather, she had all the pain and humiliation that comes with any break-up, then she had the terrifying responsibility of raising a fabulous daughter, and also embarking on a whole new chapter of her life, coming out as gay and having to navigate people's responses to that."

Clara was silent. She looked at her boots and shoved sand back and forth with them as she considered what

Ray had said.

"Yeah, I know," she finally agreed with a sigh. "And granny and grandad dying. It was a lot all at once."

"Oh," Ray said in surprise. "I didn't even know about that part."

"That's how we got the big, stupid, ugly house. She could *never* afford that on her *own*."

"What are you talking about," Ray asked with a light laugh. "That house is amazing. It's so gothic and cool, like something out of a Dickens novel – please tell me you've read some Dickens."

"Who?" Clara asked with a squint.

Ray's jaw dropped. "You must at least know the story of A Christmas Carol."

"Oh – the one with the Muppets?" Clara asked innocently.

Ray gulped. "Yes... that is *one* version of it, I suppose. I'm going to buy you some books. I can't let you get to adulthood without knowing some of the classics." Ray was shaking her head. "Anyway, back to your mum. What you just said there about her parents both dying. That's huge. She's had an enormous amount to deal with and yet she goes about town with a huge smile for everyone, looking sassy on her paddleboard and bravely coming to meet strangers in the sea. She's awesome. She's interesting. And by god, does she care about you. She's desperate to find you. I ran away once, when I was around your age because I didn't want to go back to boarding school. I hitch-hiked my way to London, which wasn't that far really from where I grew up, and I tracked down my cousin who worked at the British Museum. I stayed with her for three days before they even tried to look for me. They were so defiant, they tried to show me a lesson by ignoring me, hoping I'd come home with my tail between my legs. I'd convinced my cousin that my parents knew I was there for a course I had to attend while my cousin was out at work. Her mum – my aunt – eventually phoned and said there was a search on for me and that was it blown. They came to collect me by car the next day. They barely said a word to me all the way home. No hugs, no conversations about why I had done it. Nothing. And I was so disappointed, so empty, that I just went home with them and carried on as if nothing had happened. And, of course, I went back to boarding school like a good girl. I ran away from there a year later...but that's a story for another time."

Clara was open-mouthed as she listened.

"The point is, no good comes from running away. And you need to know how cared for you really are. You're lucky. I know you don't feel lucky just now, but I can see it. I can see how treasured you are."

Clara squinted at the ocean far below their vantage point. "I suppose she's not the worst," she eventually conceded. "She does make a really good lasagne." They both laughed.

"And Heather's great," Clara added. "I'm actually really pleased they're together. They seem really in love."

Ray asked, tentatively, "Could that be another reason you're unhappy? You feel left out?"

Clara pursed her lips and nodded, holding back tears. "They've got each other. Dad's got his girlfriend. They make all the decisions, including huge things like moving over 150 miles north to nowhere land. I don't really have a place in any of it."

Ray put an arm around Clara's shoulder. "You'll carve out your own path. You absolutely will. But for now, your role is to let your mum look after you. Trust her decisions. Enjoy the nature up here and give it time. I promise, it's not all that bad here. You can come and visit me in my little house by the bay when you want to get away from home. I have easels and a whole cupboard of paint supplies if you like art. I can teach you to meditate... whatever. Just know that you don't need to be lonely in Brogie."

Clara grinned. "I suppose my mum can't be that bad if she's making friends like you. You're slaying it."

Ray laughed. "Yep. I'm slaying life. I was actually on a hot date tonight. He's freezing his balls off just over there, waiting for us."

"Oops." Clara exclaimed. "I've ruined your night."

Ray shook her head. "No, no. You've done me a favour. I always move way too fast with men. Thank you for causing this whole drama and putting the brakes on my love life."

They both laughed. Clara was like a different girl with her anger diffused and the ability to open up to conversation. Her eyes sparkled in the silver light.

"Shall we walk up that steep hill to your super cool mansion?" Ray asked.

"OK," Clara agreed. "I wasn't really enjoying this anyway," she added with a whisper. "They're so drunk on this awful kiwi stuff and one guy kept flashing his butt – like I want to see *that*."

CHAPTER 21 – THE DEAD SEA

I t was a misty morning. The forecast had promised sunshine, but there was a thick harr lazing about on the surface of the water, not looking keen to move on any time soon.

"I think it's rather beautiful," said Ray with a breezy voice.

Brydie stood, hands on hips, examining the water. "Yeah, it's quite mystical. You can't even see the other side of the bay, never mind the horizon. It's like we're lost." She shot a mischievous faux-afraid expression in Ray's direction.

Martha pulled up in her red car and marched quickly towards the slipway with an air of urgency. "Sorry I'm late," she gushed.

"No worries," Brydie said, exuding calmness. "We're in no hurry."

"Any sign of Kim?" Ray asked, looking directly at Brydie.

"I honestly don't know," she responded meekly, her tone changing from calm to concerned. She added: "I texted her, but she hasn't replied yet."

The three women were finally stripped of their thick outer layers and about to plod, nervously, down the slipway. The group's nerves hadn't died down yet as they knew that the moment their skin hit the water there would be a sharp shock. They still had to encourage each other and summon all their courage to wade in.

"Wait for me!" Kim called. "I only have an hour before work, but I've missed too many swims."

She threw her bag, with its easy to identify colourful sugar skull motif and bright blue changing robe on the concrete ground at the top of the slipway and breathlessly stepped in time with the others. Brydie glanced back at her with an awkward smile.

Kim gingerly returned the smile. It was like an unspoken pact between the two of them to move on. Brydie's grin grew wide as she turned back to face the water.

The four usual suspects yelped and gasped as they stepped deeper and deeper into the calm water, which if Brydie's flash watch was accurate, was sitting at ten degrees on this misty morning.

The women were shoulder-deep, breathing heavily between laughter and commenting on the sumptuous silvery-grey reflection on the water's top layer because of the mist.

A man's voice rang out from the direction of the harbour. He sprinted closer and closer until they could make out his uniform and face.

"It's Gordon from the coastguard," Kim said in confusion.

"Hi ladies," he shouted, now that he was close enough to peer down from the stone wall just past the slipway. "I don't think it's a good idea to be swimming round here today."

"Oh?" Martha asked, as the others all eyed each other in uncertainty.

"Keep this under wraps, but, there's a search on," he confided, checking behind his shoulder. "A young lad is missing," he continued. "Suspected jumper at four in the morning."

The group let out gasps and small murmurs of shock.

"Jesus," Ray whispered.

"The tide suggests he could have washed up in this direction," Gordon said as sensitively as he could from up high on the wall. "I wouldn't want you to come across anything you don't want to be seeing, if you know what I mean."

They nodded. "Of course," Brydie said respectfully.

He gave a wave of thanks and ran back in the direction he came from.

The dookers were quiet. The mood had well and truly plummeted. The tingling of their skin was the last thing on their minds.

"We should really get out now," Martha said, her eyes wide with worry. "I wonder who the poor guy is."

The cool water around their bodies no longer seemed inviting. "It feels disrespectful being here when there's something like that going on," Kim said softly. She was met with nods of agreement as they all turned and gracefully tiptoed on the seabed back to the slipway.

As they got dried and dressed, there was none of the usual hilarity and jokes about overgrown pubes or topping up their layers of protective blubber with post-swim cake. The mood was extremely solemn. They could see several vehicles parked over at the harbour, a mixture of coastguard and police. People in high visibility waterproofs were darting about, swiftly dealing with equipment and the sounds of engines could be heard echoing around the area as inflatable motorboats were returning and others were setting off. It was a rare and disturbing scene in the usually peaceful bay.

They said their goodbyes fairly quickly, over their steaming travel mugs, not wanting to appear uncaring or ignorant to the drama surrounding their adopted swim spot.

"Wait a second Kim," Brydie called out softly after her friend. "Can we have a chat sometime? I don't want to leave things like they were."

Kim's face eased. "Yeah, I think we should. I've got no kids tonight, if you're free. My mum is having them for a sleepover."

"You don't have plans for your child free night?" Brydie asked curiously.

Kim awkwardly brushed past the comment with an assertive "no".

"Great," Brydie said, forcing a lightness into her voice. "Pop over for a drink. I need one after the week we've had with the kids. It's supposed to be a lovely night. We could sit outside."

"Sounds like a plan," Kim said as she picked up her swim bag. "See you then."

Brydie was the last to leave. She turned to look at the floating layer of mist once more, wondering who the lost man was and where he would end up. "Poor dude," she muttered as she began her short walk home, warming up under the waterproof-coated changing robe which gave a satisfying swishing noise with each movement of her arms. Sort of like the swishing of the waves. Noticing this detail made Brydie smile ever so slightly, glad to avert her thoughts from the possible suicide in their beloved waters.

Later that evening, Brydie was sitting at a small bistro table and chairs set in the front garden, sipping her first glass of chardonnay. She stretched her legs out. It had been a funny week. Full of ill feeling and sickness and now a stark reminder of mortality with the day's activity. Her front garden looked over the sea, from a different perspective to the cottages down by the bay. The village jutted out into the ocean as a peninsula. While Ray's cottage faced west, Brydie's faced east. It made for a completely contrasting mood of ocean. Some days it could be calm as a Buddhist monk at the bay but wild as a roaring lion at the back shore and vice versa.

Tonight, however, Brydie's view was of calm, still water and a clear sky. Summer was well and truly edging forward. In a few hours the sky would be bloodshot red and orange as the sun made its dramatic exit. It was one of Brydie's absolute favourite things about her view and she was looking forward to taking in that sight with Kim and a bottle or two to share. Like old times. It would fix all the weirdness between them, Brydie hoped.

She could see Kim strolling down the street from her cottage a few doors up. They gave each other a keen wave each and by the time Kim arrived she was grinning. Brydie leapt out of her chair and threw her arms around Kim. The pair were stuck together with invisible Velcro for a few minutes, before breaking apart and sighing with happy relief.

"I'm sorry about the other day," Brydie said, wanting to get the inevitable out of the way. "It's nothing to do with me what you and Rick are doing. You have kids together, for goodness sake. I need to leave you to work this out on your own."

Kim smiled in gratitude and responded: "Hey, I'm sorry too. I flew off the handle at you and said some things I regret. I know you were just worried about me after all I've said about him. I'm not really sure what's happening between us…but it's worth giving it a go…I think. I'll go with the flow."

Without saying another word, Brydie carefully poured a glass of wine for Kim and handed it over as if it was an Oscar, shining and golden.

Kim's eyes lit up. "Oh my god, do I need this!" she declared. "It was horrendous in the café today. It was so busy and I just couldn't be bothered. People were in a really funny mood. Do you think it's been a full moon or something?"

"It's probably to do with the young guy that's missing," Brydie said, staring out at the stretch of mirror-like water leading to the hills way off in the distance.

"Of course," Kim said, shaking her head at the memory of some awful revelations. "People were talking about it in the kitchen at work."

"Oh really?" Brydie said, sitting forward a little, desperate for information.

"You know Maggie who works in the shop?" Kim asked. Brydie nodded. "It's her son. Twenty-four years old."

"Woah," Brydie said, putting her hand over her gaping mouth. "Poor Maggie."

"Apparently last night he left a goodbye message online then just left his house with no belongings – no phone, no watch, no jacket. He just walked out. He lived with his girlfriend and she didn't even know he was gone until she woke up this morning. Imagine how awful that must be."

They sat in silence for a few moments. The depth of the news sinking in. Kim continued: "He always seemed so happy, when I would see him around. I didn't know him that well, but he always said hi. Maggie was always telling people in the shop about his rugby achievements or that she was hoping for wedding bells."

"You just never know what's going on in someone's mind," Brydie said, eyeing the pale straw-coloured liquid in her glass. "You just wish you could rewind the world and get to him before he did anything and show him that nothing is worth doing that. Whatever was going on for him...there must have been some way to fix it or make it more bearable at least. No twenty-four-year-old should get to that stage, where there feels like no other option. It's horrible."

The calm summer evening sounds filled the air around the two sad women as they sat, quietly sipping. The reliably ever-present sound of birds singing melodies to each other was a welcome comfort.

Another noise attracted the women's attention towards the sea. At this side of the village there was no beach running alongside the water, only rugged rocks and plunging depths. A motorised fishing boat slowed to a stop and cut its engine. Two men on the boat stood together at the side facing land, hands on hips, looking into the water. One man went into the small cabin, leaving the other man watching something on his own.

Brydie and Kim looked at each other anxiously. "You don't think it could be....?" Brydie trailed off as the pair watched in anticipation.

Nothing happened for a few minutes. Brydie and Kim could barely tear their eyes away and it didn't feel like the right time to launch into a new conversation.

A bright orange rib boat drew close to the fishing boat calmly, obviously not wanting to cause big waves and slowed to a stop. The men from each boat began a discussion, looking down into the water together solemnly as their vessels bobbed up and down gently. Before long, the coastguard men from the orange boat were reaching down into the water and yanking something up. Brydie and Kim both winced and turned their heads away after seeing the stiff body of the young man being dragged out of the water and onto the boat. Kim grabbed Brydie's hand and squeezed. "Poor, poor boy," she whispered.

In only minutes, the boats both left the scene and headed west to navigate the corner and find the harbour entrance.

All that was left at the point where the body was recovered were a few residual waves from the trail of the boats. It was as if nothing had happened. The sea continued its constant movement, an innocent, yet vital, character in this traumatic act. The birds sang relentlessly, oblivious to the loss of a young life. And Brydie and Kim sat stunned, clutching their wine glasses, paused, as if it was wrong to press play on their, generally, happy lives again.

CHAPTER 22 – BRYDIE

Two weeks after dark tragedy had crept through the village, the Brogie Bay Dookers were planning to turn the bay neon for one night only. In the 'dooks' since the coastguard drama, the women had set about planning a charity solstice swim which they hoped would raise some cash to pour back into the coastguard service, as well as a men's mental health charity.

They spewed ideas at Brydie and she relished taking up the role of party planner. She thrived on this sort of organisation. Her kitchen table was out of bounds for the rest of the household until after June twenty-first. There were neat lists of items needed, such as charity buckets, floodlights borrowed from the coastguard – they were going to have to earn their monetary donation it seemed, but they were more than keen – food suppliers and hundreds of glowsticks.

The food suppliers' list was the most heart-warming. Brydie kept having to scribble spider leg lines tailing off her list to various food donations that kept being offered: home bakes from some women in the village; BBQ food donated by the butcher and cooked by Mike and a colleague on the night; the village hall committee were going to bring vats of hot tea and paper cups; Ray and Kim offered to make flasks of hot mulled cider; and the local ice cream van was going to turn up and offer a percentage of proceeds to the charity total. It was all coming together.

Kim had a friend who wrote for the local paper in the

nearest big town and said she'd try and get the event covered.

Finally, Brydie had bought hundreds of glow sticks and spent a whole evening sticking the little plastic fasteners onto them so it would be easier for people to make bracelets or necklaces. Doug kept trying to convince her it was fine to leave it for people to do it themselves but Brydie was in way too deep already. She felt she had a significant purpose. What she wasn't going to tell Doug was that she'd also used her credit card to buy some champagne for the core group of Dookers and plastic wine goblets with 'solstice vibes' printed on them to give to the group as a memento. He only got fed information on what he could *actually see* on the kitchen table. The bubbly and goblets were already stashed in the boot safely...and secretly.

The big day – solstice – finally arrived and Brydie had a definite spring in her step. The Dookers were doing something important. They were supporting a vital service. And from what she'd heard in the shop, there were going to be quite a few new swimmers joining them for a one-off experience. The coastguard was also going to bring first aid kits and spare blankets, and voluntarily stay up late to watch the midnight event with their huge lights shining down onto the water for safety.

Brydie felt occasional whooshes of nerves in her stomach at the responsibility of it all.

"What if it's really shit?" she asked Doug over a cup of green tea on the sofa that afternoon. "I'll look like an absolute tit if hardly anyone turns up and we're left with loads of wasted food and we hardly raise any money."

"I doubt very much that's going to happen," he said, placing his hand on her knee. "I've heard quite a few people saying they're keen. I nearly dropped my sausages in the shop yesterday when I heard the dreaded Dora saying she might do it."

"Doug! Be nice. She's not dreaded," Brydie said, slapping his forearm gently. She continued: "Yes, she drives on the pavements sometimes because she's got the patience of a... what has no patience....a greyhound once it's been let out of the starting cage thingy...."

"Or a piranha dropped into a kids' swimming pool," Doug added.

Brydie's eyes sparkled and she offered: "Or a randy old perve who's just been handed a stack of notes in a strip club."

Doug took the metaphoric baton once more and said: "Or a... seagull when you walk out of the chippy with an open cone of chips."

"Anyway," Brydie interjected, still giggling. "Poor Dora. I feel sorry for her. She may have been around all the men her age in the village, but she's alright really."

"I'd better watch myself," Doug mocked. "I'm near enough her age bracket – she'll maybe have a go at pulling me next."

Brydie looked him up and down with an air of mock disapproval before saying: "Nah. I don't think you need to worry."

Doug let out a hearty laugh, grabbed a cushion from behind him and threw it towards her.

Brydie shrieked and batted it to the floor. "Kidding!" She cried. "You've got the hottest dad bod in the village. You're a hottie. Anyway, back to Dora – I think she's mysterious. She's always just on the right side of tipsy and her eyes bore into you like she has powers beyond our comprehension. It's like... there's a lot more to her than we think and she's probably had a really interesting life." Doug stared at Brydie in amazement. "Your ability to see THE best in everyone never fails to stun me," he said. "And that's one of the reasons I love you."

Brydie grinned, slightly sarcastically. "Well, I am pretty feckin' special," she teased, before picking up her phone for a quick browse on the socials and to see if there were any new responses to her post about the event.

"Oh. Wow. It's Martha's birthday tomorrow. We should sing happy birthday to her at midnight." Her eyes lit up with excitement. Surprise acts of kindness were her catnip. As if fuelled by that idea, she leapt up off the sofa.

"I'm going to go and get my outfit ready for tonight," she declared.

"But you're not meeting people down there until ten tonight," Doug said, bewildered.

"Yes, but, I can't sit here all day listening to you slag people off," she said, then gave a mischievous wink and left the room dramatically for effect. She called over her shoulder as she walked down the hallway: "I've got to go and pick up the trestle tables we're borrowing from the community hall. Maybe there's a really nice strong man who wouldn't mind helping me with that....?"

"Ask Dora!" he retorted. "She knows plenty of them." Then a minute later, after heaving himself off the comfy sofa, he shouted out: "I'm on my way!"

CHAPTER 23 – MARTHA

"**I** can't believe I'm fifty-nine tomorrow," she said, rolling onto her side to face Ron. He took out the bite guard he wore every night to prevent him from grinding his teeth and shoved it in his glass of water on the bedside table.

"Yeah. It's not quite the big one yet," he replied with an eyebrow raise. "I'll have to start thinking about the big six-oh and what to do."

"Never mind next year," Martha said, "I hope you've prepared something nice for *this* year."

Ron smiled. "Of course I have. You'll have to wait and see. It's lucky you're not working tomorrow so we can spend the day together."

"It's not luck," Martha explained. "I book my birthday off every year, you wally."

Ron rolled his eyes and grabbed at Martha's waist under the covers. "You don't flinch so much now," he commented. "It's really nice. Something's changed."

Martha looked up at the ceiling in thought before responding: "I guess, baring all in a swimsuit with new people has helped me get over my body. Even when people walk past us as we're walking down the slip with it all hanging out, I really don't care."

"That's great," Ron said, clearly enjoying sinking his fingers into Martha's rolls.

"And getting older," she continued, "I'm realising how many years I've wasted feeling fat and gross. I mean, really, who cares? What's it stopping me from doing?

Nothing. The girls in the group don't bat an eyelid at my wobbly thighs, in fact, they point out their own wobbles. I'm realising we've all got bits we don't like, but at the end of the day, it's just bodies. I'm using my body for joy now."

Ron gave a chuckle.

"No, not in *that* way," Martha retorted, before he could slip in a naughty joke. "It's as if the sea and my body are both teaching me that I can do exciting things, *feel* exciting things, with the body I've got. OK, I've got my aches, but they could be a lot worse. My hip gets stiff and sore, yeah, but not when I'm in cold water. It's like a magic potion that wipes away my aches and my self-consciousness."

Ron was straight-faced now. "I'm really glad you've joined this group," he said, clasping her hand in his and pulling it up to his mouth to gently kiss her knuckles. "It's doing wonderful things to you. Just don't expect me to be jumping in the Moray Firth. I spent my youth training how to survive a fall in the sea for the fishing boats. We did everything we could to *avoid* plunging in."

Martha laughed and rolled her eyes. "I think falling into deep waters off the side of a boat is just a little bit more extreme than walking into shoulder-deep, calm water just off the bay. You'd probably love it."

Ron shook his head adamantly.

"Besides," she added with a flicker of naughtiness flushing over her face, "I don't want you to come. You'd cramp my style with my new friends."

Later that day, Martha was packing her swim bag. It was becoming habitual. It always made her feel a rush of positive anticipation. Packing her neoprene boots and gloves into the bag, along with a flask and woolly bobble hat in case there was a chilly wind that day, reminded her of what was to come. Socialising with the others was as much a part of the appeal as the cold water benefits. She felt so at ease with this little band of nature-lovers, more so than any group she'd joined before. The crochet group were too focused on attention to detail and Martha had been bored out of her brain on the first night. The salsa tutor was too saucy and kept grabbing her hips, trying to force them into a sexy swaying motion, which was just not Martha's bag. A painful week at outdoor bowling was enough for her to never want to bend over again. And the only time she ever wanted to roll a bowling ball again would be to roll it into the fires of hell. But wading into chilly water regularly and laughing until her stomach muscles hurt was the best therapy in an otherwise stressful life of worrying about her parents and tiredness from cleaning busy hospital wards.

For this evening's swim, however, the bag packing was a little different. Not only was there a theme of bright coloured swimsuits, which gave Martha a nice excuse to treat herself to a bright orange and neon pink mermaid scales number (with reinforced "suck me in" fabric at the waist), but she also had some light-up disco ball earrings and neon face paint in there too. It felt like she was preparing for a night out...in the sea. This was definitely a new experience.

She also had a little surprise for the four other core members of the group. She tucked five pairs of glittery, bright pink mittens she'd knitted throughout the build-up to the event into a side pocket of her bag. She, and the four others, could warm up their cold fingers after the dook, but in style.

Having a focus had brought back the first glimpse of creative spark in a long time. Martha was energised.

The group weren't meeting until ten, to help Brydie get things set up for people arriving from 11pm onwards. Looking at the clock, Martha dashed back to the kitchen to grab a pasta bake she'd made for her mum and dad and drove the five-minute journey to their bungalow up on the hill just above the village.

It was a stunning day. Clear skies and just a hint of a breeze. She stood outside her parked car for a moment, taking in the scene. The village below looked cute. The dark bluey, grey slate roof tiles ran in rows above grey stone cottages and painted cottages in shades of white, yellow and pale blue. At either side of the long, straight village, the sea lapped away at the land gently – at one side, the harbour and sandy bay, at the other side a vast stretch of water leading to the hills of the northern highlands in the distance. Martha never grew tired of this view. Her parents had moved up to this little house on the hill after the kids – Martha and her brother Jack – had grown up. Jack died several years ago after being struck by a car whilst riding his beloved Harley Davidson on winding roads, travelling west towards Gairloch on a sunny day. Martha's mum and dad had never been the same since. She believed the trauma set off her father's dementia. And the stress of that had triggered a slight breakdown in her mother's mental health. They were lost, but lost together.

Still holding the warm dish of cheesy, vegetable pasta bake in her hands, she looked over to her left, past this little housing estate and to the mansion set back from all other houses in its own grounds, powerful and bold above the rest of civilisation. She'd always loved the dramatic old building but now it felt very different, knowing that a young family were desperately trying to breathe life back into the old place. Lisa's presence on the hill gave it a more homely feel. It was no longer a mysterious, ramshackle, lonely old house.

With a soft smile, Martha turned and went inside.

"Mum, dad! I've got dinner for you," she called out.

Martha's mum marched into the hallway. "It's not a good day to come, dear," her mother said, grabbing her by the elbow, spinning her back round to the front door and escorting her off the premises. "Your father's naked," she said, quite sternly, barely changing her facial expression.

"What? Can't you give him a dressing gown or something?" Martha asked in confusion.

"No," her mum said, matter-of-factly.

There was silence, while Martha waited for more detail, which never came. She shook her head as if to clear her muddled thoughts. "OK, well, here's some food for you anyway."

Her mother reached out for the glass dish and said a polite thank you, still barely changing her expression.

"Are you OK?" Martha asked. "Would you like me to come in and speak to dad? I could help you dress him, or…"

"No, darling," her mother said with an heir of superiority. "We've got the carer coming at seven and she's *very* good with him. He's convinced his clothes are suffocating him today. He's quite happy otherwise."

"Ok," Martha said, a little hurt that the carer took top priority over his own daughter. "So… shall I just go? I was going to stay and eat with you both." She eyed the pasta bake.

"That was a lovely idea," her mother said, stiffly. "Another time perhaps." And with that, she gave a forced smile, a small nod and closed the door, leaving Martha on the doorstep, dumbstruck.

"Well, at least you've got a good meal," she muttered to herself and vowed to call the carer soon to check in on how things were from her point of view.

Martha could feel her shoulders and chest were tight from stress. She was frozen on the doorstep wondering if it was really okay to just leave. If she forced herself into the home to 'help', surely it would cause more distress. But was she doing enough?

She took a deep breath in and closed her eyes, turning back towards her car. When she exhaled and opened her eyes, the comforting view of the coast marginally eased her tension and she rolled her shoulders to soften her stance.

After eating a quick dinner of sausages and rice – which was highly disappointing to Martha after the let down of not getting to share the gorgeously crusty cheese-topped pasta bake she'd so lovingly created – it was time to head down to the slip to start setting up.

CHAPTER 24 – THE SOLSTICE DOOK

The summer sky was peachy-hued as the sun was preparing to hand over to its more subtle colleague, the moon, for a short period of mood lighting. At this halfway point in the year in northern Scotland, the moon barely has to clock in for more than a few hours, leaving all the hard work to the sun.

There was a buzz of excitement between the Dookers as they set up tables and laid out plastic tubs full of home baked goodies. Brydie had designed labels for the charity buckets and had one on each table for villagers to pay whatever they wanted to for the treats.

Mike arrived with two large, metal barbecues, and the help of his burly friend Phil, who was wearing a BBQ King Apron and a proud grin that communicated the idea "fret not, the King is here".

Ray teased "Long live the King!" as she passed him and curtseyed as much as she could with two huge flasks cradled in each arm. "This is the precious mulled cider," she oozed with a mischievous grin.

"For *after* the swim!" Brydie chimed in as she breezed past, eyes down, examining at a list. "No dooking under the influence of alcohol."

Kim added in a loud whisper: "At least not tonight, with the whole village and the coastguard crew watching." She winked at Ray as she helped set out the flasks and towers of paper cups. Brydie appeared at their backs and said coyly: "I actually have something for later."

She held out a cardboard box for the two women to inspect and as their eyes fell on three bottles of champagne and the Solstice Vibes goblets their expressions melted into joyous gratitude.

"Oh Bry, that's amazing," Kim said, reaching her arms over the box to embrace her friend.

"Those are just for us group members, so we'll hide them under the table in case anyone helps themselves. That champagne is to toast the group and Martha's birthday." She checked over her shoulder, but Martha was busy hanging fabric bunting along the railings of the esplanade which ran alongside their beloved slipway.

With everything in place, including the ice cream van and the plumes of smoke as Mike and Phil began to work their magic, it was less than an hour until midnight.

"Here, put these on," Kim said, offering Ray a necklace made of neon glow sticks. "And these…" She handed her a pair of fake glasses which were luminescent blue.

Ray duly adopted the accessories and began dancing around the grassy area in a fluorescent yellow tutu over a tie-dye swimsuit, surrounded by the goodies tables.

"Music!" Brydie exclaimed. "Damn. I'll text Doug."

Adorned with neon everything – necklaces, bracelets, earrings, tiaras, glasses, and brightly-coloured swimming gear, Brydie, Kim, Ray, Martha and Lisa posed for a few photographs for the newspaper photographer with the light fading fast and the sky turning violet.

Martha turned to Lisa excitedly and whispered: "This is insane. I've never done anything like this before."

Brydie was busy explaining to the news reporter that she'd bought "eco-friendly" glow sticks when Ray passed on her way to the barbecues.

"How's it going over here?" she asked Mike, inspecting the sizzling burgers.

"Awesome," he replied, catching her eye and then looking down at the burgers quickly.

"Is there anything vegetarian?" she asked, not looking too hopeful.

"Of course," Mike said with a charming smile. "Jock – the butcher – thinks of everything. Veggie burgers are on Phil's grill."

"Ooh," Ray's eyes lit up. She browsed her purse for a handful of coins to throw in the bucket, which made a low thudding noise as they hit the bottom of the, so far, empty bucket. "I'll take one of those please Phil."

As she bit into the roll, her eyes met Mike's and they laughed. Phil looked at Mike, then back at Ray, then back at Mike as if the penny was dropping that something was going on here.

With her bite eventually chewed and swallowed, Ray said: "That is a seriously good burger. By the way, Mike, you left your jacket at mine yesterday."

"Oh yes, I realised that after I got home," he replied, stifling a laugh. "It was a little late, and I was... you know... a bit worse for wear."

Ray chuckled. "Yes, you were going to go home and write a song about a lost love letter in your post bag. How did that go?"

Mike's smile widened as he placed his palm on the side of his face, aware of the heat radiating from his blush. "Not very well. I got home and fell asleep on the sofa."

"It was a very good night anyway," Ray said, looking at her burger intently with a smirk. "And no interruptions to go and join a search party this time."

"Indeed," Mike grinned, and as Ray glanced up at him

he held her gaze firmly with his.

"Alright, alright, knock it off you two," Phil joked. "It's making me feel a bit ill, all this flirting."

Ray gave them both a little wave and made her way back to Kim and the others, who were now mingling with villagers. In the short time it had taken Ray to buy a burger...and do a little flirting... at least twenty people had gathered on the grass, all chatting and buying up teas, coffees and cakes. It was a warm night, for the north of Scotland anyway, and the mix of scents in the air of ocean, sizzling food and coffee were intoxicating. They held a promise of good times and brought back memories for Ray of various festivals and summer adventures. She watched the growing crowd happily as Doug appeared in his car, waving at Brydie and shouting: "Don't worry, I'm on it!"

He ran an extension cable from the coastguard shed to the tables and plugged in an enormous speaker. A few moments of tapping on his phone and some disco classics began floating out, lifting the atmosphere instantly.

Brydie ran to him and gave him a huge kiss on the lips. Ray watched with fondness how the couple kept physical contact while chatting to the others. Doug's hand remained around Brydie's waist while she kept one hand on his arm, throwing back her head to laugh at something someone had said to the couple.

Lisa appeared, her golden, wavy hair down for once, giving nervous waves to the five women she knew and sought out Ray like a magnet for safety. "Hi," she said in a breathless, almost nervous tone.

"Hey beautiful," Ray said warmly. "How are you?"

Lisa rolled her eyes. "A lot better than the other night. Thank you so much for finding Clara and bringing her home. She really likes you. You made a good impression. I was in such a state I didn't really thank you enough. It would be lovely if you could come up to the house for a glass of wine or dinner...so I can thank you properly."

"There's no need to thank me," Ray said, "I'm just glad we could help."

"Well, come up for...a social night," Lisa ventured tentatively. "It would be nice to get to know you better."

"I'd absolutely love that," Ray replied with a nod. "Message me so we can arrange it. Make sure you get some champagne after the swim. And some of my mulled cider – it has a rum kick!"

It was fifteen minutes to midnight. Brydie stood on a crate with her back to the sea, facing the large crowd who had now arrived. To her delight dozens of people were there in swimming gear – some in thick wetsuits, others in swimsuits under thick coats, raring to take the plunge with the Dookers. Even her mum, Sally, had turned up to watch – in a faux fur-trimmed winter coat and high-heeled boots...definitely not planning on entering the sea. She gave Brydie a thumbs up from the crowd.

Phil chimed his beer bottle with his grilling fork, prompting everyone to hush and turn their attention to Brydie.

She gave Phil a thank you nod and cleared her throat. "Ahem. Thank you, everyone, for coming. It's amazing to see so many of you. We weren't sure what to expect. Obviously, the main reason we wanted to do something organised like this was to raise money for the amazing coastguard for all that they do. Obviously, there was a devastating call out for the team recently, but they also work tirelessly all year round."

The crowd began to clap in the direction of the

coastguard team, who were manning the portable floodlight pillar.

Brydie grinned at Doug and waited for the crowd to settle again. "The other charity we are sharing proceeds from tonight with is about men's mental health. If we can do anything to help stop another family going through what has happened to one family in this village recently, it will be money well spent." There was more applause.

Maggie came forward from behind a cluster of people, which took Brydie by surprise. "I'm so grateful for what you're doing tonight," she said, her voice breaking with waves of emotion. "I wouldn't wish the pain of suicide on any family. We need to raise awareness and give money to help other young men like my Dylan."

Brydie's eyes were dewy with tears. She gulped and held her hands in a prayer gesture towards Maggie. The crowd gently applauded once more and people who clearly knew Maggie very well gathered round her offering hugs as she broke down.

Maggie left with a woman and a young man after stuffing some cash into one of the buckets and giving Brydie a delicate wave.

Brydie was still on the crate and, sensing this was the right moment, she declared. "So... let's fill those buckets for good causes, but now it's time to get in that...very dark...sea and celebrate the longest day of the year! I don't know much about solstice, but I did read something rather lovely about it being the time of the year when light defeats dark. Let's celebrate lightness. It's solstice swim time!"

Doug rushed to her to give her a kiss as she stepped off the crate and gushed: "Well done, gorgeous. I've never seen you do anything like that."

Brydie clutched her chest. "Was it alright? Did I say the right things?"

"Hell, yeah," he declared.

It was time for the swimmers to walk down the slipway into the water, casting unearthly neon reflections across the silky, black water.

Martha's mouth was open in awe. "It's so beautiful seeing all the lights reflecting," she gasped. The glitter body paint she had smeared on her cheeks in heart shapes glistened in the glow of the floodlight as she grinned at her buddies and yelped as the cold water snatched upwards at her lower back.

The five core women held hands as they walked further out to reach bust depth in the water, giggling and shrieking all the way. But the most awe-inspiring moment was turning in each direction to see neon glowing in all directions. There were at least fifty people joining them that night in the salty water. It was incredible.

"Hold on!" came a cry from dry land and they turned to see Mike running towards the water, a glowing pair of glasses adorning his deliriously happy face as he splashed down the slip fully clothed. "I'm not missing this!"

Ray gasped and applauded him. "Go Mikey!"

He splashed a clumsy run all the way to her, held her firmly by the shoulders and planted a meaningful kiss on her lips. The other group members let out whoops and laughter and teasing "oooh"s at the romantic gesture. When Mike eventually pulled back from the kiss, he looked like a boy who'd scored the winning goal for his school football team. The pride, and the passion, oozed from him into the water, surrounding the pair like a rainbow-coloured oil slick.

Brydie's eyes were fixed on her waterproof watch as she shouted out into the night air: "It's countdown time. Ten, nine..."

Voices rang out all around her as the rest of the countdown flowed across the water surface. "four, three, two, one..."

Cheers and whoops gave way to the song "Happy birthday to you," as Brydie led the surprise gesture with her hand extended towards Martha. Everyone followed suit – even the thirty or so onlookers from dry land – including Ron, who had come down to watch the event.

Martha's mouth dropped open as she glanced from dooker to dooker in awe, tears forming in her eyes, causing the neon lights to merge into bursts of blurry colour in her vision.

When the song ended, Martha rushed at Brydie, making an impressive splash and threw her arms around her. "Thank you so much," she gushed. "I'll never forget that. That was just....incredible. To be sung to at midnight in the sea by so many people. Wow." She wiped tears from her cheeks, which smeared glitter in all directions.

The main members of the Dookers gave her birthday hugs one by one, showing that while they'd only known each other for several weeks, they'd formed some pretty special bonds in this body of water. The conversations they'd had over the weeks whilst dodging blooms of stray seaweed or jumping the occasional wave that came roaring towards them had been personal and cathartic, about every aspect of life. Their bonds were sealed.

Aware of it being even colder in the absence of sunlight, the group sensibly led their throng of swim guests out to dry land after only ten minutes and shoved on warm layers before popping corks and pouring steaming cider into paper cups.

Martha's glitter mittens went down a storm and Kim asked someone to take a picture of them all holding their goblets full of champers whilst wearing the bright pink mittens – which made for some near-misses and cries of "don't waste the champagne!" as the goblets slipped around in their woolly grasps.

Martha declared: "I'm getting tipsy! I don't usually drink. It's my birthday!"

Ron edged into the circle and introduced himself. Martha held up her goblet to his mouth, practically forcing him to take a gulp of bubbly, which made the others laugh.

Martha patted his nose with her mitten and giggled: "I think the birthday girl wants to be wooed tonight."

Ron's eyes grew wide and he announced: "I'm glad I wore my lucky pants tonight. I knew they'd work." He flashed a wink at the group and began laughing as Martha threw her arms around his neck, a bit on the heavy side, causing him to stumble backwards, before steadying his footing.

Brydie felt a tap on the shoulder and turned around to see her mum.

"Well done, darling," Sally said. "This has been really impressive. I'm going home now because I'm freezing and I'm going away to Edinburgh shopping tomorrow, but have a lovely night." She kissed her daughter's cheek and pulled away to head for home.

"Thanks, mum," Brydie called after her. "That means a lot!" She smiled as she watched her mum walk away, taken aback that she'd even come along to something like this.

There was a real buzz of achievement as people sipped from cups and ate caramel shortcake and muffins and talked about the experience, which for dozens of them was brand new. As Brydie walked from the Dookers over to Doug, who was now helping pack up the retired barbecue, she picked up parts of conversations, such as: "I can't believe I got in there tonight, it was so cold, but so fun" and "I might start dooking more often, I feel pumped".

She grinned from ear to ear as she stopped and took in the atmosphere of the entire event. Happy faces, punctuated by neon lights and charity buckets which were now heavy to lift made all those lists and all the fretting worthwhile. She looked out to the almost black night ocean, where only a tiny hint of summer light whispered at the horizon and did 'a Ray'. She whispered: "Thank you universe, for all of this. Thanks for the swims, thanks for the people. Thanks for the hope."

CHAPTER 25 – KIM

I t was the morning after the Solstice Dook. Evidence of the event lay strewn on Kim's oak-effect bedside table – several plastic sticks without the glow, some huge star-shaped earrings, her solstice goblet, with a hint of dried-up cider at the bottom.

Her mum had stayed over with the kids, which accounted for the banging and clattering noises floating through the hallway from the kitchen.

Kim blinked several times until her eyes were ready to open and stare at the comfortingly plain white ceiling. Bacon. The scent of smoked bacon rashers under the grill filled Kim's nostrils with pleasure. *Good old mum*, she thought. She could hear Stan chatting at double speed to his granny but she couldn't make out the words – in fairness, even in the same room it could be difficult to make out the content of his super-excited verbal babble.

Thudding footsteps sped along the wooden hallway towards her bedroom and the door flew open.

"I have baaaaacoonnn!!" Stan bellowed proudly, holding out a plate with a seeded bun crammed with deep pink, crispy bacon. "For yooooooou."

Kim, sat up as quickly as her weary body would allow and flashed a beaming smile at her boy. "Wow, thank you! Did you help to cook it?"

Stan looked astounded. "No. I just a little boy. Granny hotted it up." He stepped forward gently like a ring bearer at a Royal wedding, intent on delivering his precious offering without a hiccup. As soon as the plate was safely in his mother's hands, he turned on his heel at lightning speed and raced back down the hallway without a second glance.

Kim shook her head, laughing, and then eyed the bacon roll with pure hunger-lust. This would be the magic cure. She wasn't hung over. A few glasses of champagne and one large cider weren't enough to make her suffer. It must have been general tiredness from work and kids, she decided, as she sank her teeth into the bun for the first mouth-watering bite. It had been a while since the smoky flavour of bacon had coated her taste buds. Working at the Beach Hut didn't exactly give her the free-flowing funds to fill the fridge with exciting goods. It was white label cheapness all the way.

Gigi appeared at the door and leaned against its frame, arms folded. "How late did you get home last night? I never got to kiss you good night."

"Jesus," Kim remarked, with a mouth full of bread and bacon. "Huge apologies for not abandoning my event to come and tuck you in."

Gigi rolled her eyes and turned to leave, but Kim instantly regretted her tone and called her back.

"Sorry, sweetie," she said, scrunching her eyes closed. "I didn't mean to be grumpy. It's just... it sometimes feels like you're the mum, disapproving of me. I hardly ever go out. Maybe once a month, to Brydie's house. And this was a really important, really exciting event. We raised money for charity. It's going in the paper."

Kim was grinning at Gigi now and patting the bedspread, inviting her to sit.

Gigi trotted over, clearly delighted to be welcomed in.

"Can I have a bite?" she asked, her eyes fixed on the glistening bacon.

"Did granny not make you a roll?" Kim asked, in confusion.

"I didn't want one. I wanted cereal."

Kim rolled her eyes. "Fine. A little bite," she said, holding it out, "but next time, don't say no. You always do that and regret it."

Gigi grinned, satisfied with just a taste. Then, a flash of excitement ran through her as she asked: "Are we going to dad's today? I can't wait to sleep at nana's tonight with dad. She's got a new set of bunk beds for me and Stan. It's going to be so cool."

Kim swallowed and felt a tummy flip of nerves, remembering the day's plans, and replied: "Oh cool. Bunk beds are fun. Yes. He's coming at one for you. I'd better get up and showered, so I'm ready for him."

"Why do *you* have to be ready? We can just run to the car. You don't have to shower for that," Gigi pointed out.

Kim was silent. She looked out the window, hoping the words for some excuse for getting dressed up would float by. They didn't. Outsmarted by a seven-year-old.

"It's just nice to be clean," she finally muttered and continued her breakfast.

Later on, after her mum had left to go and start digging her latest project of home grown tatties in the garden, Kim was sitting in the living room, with a coffee, anxiously glancing out the window every few minutes. It was five past one. She had a chewing gum pellet in her pocket to get rid of 'coffee tongue' in an instant… should there be any mouth on mouth action. Things had been picking up steadily between them. Just two nights before he'd stayed until 2am, rekindling the spark over a few glasses of wine and their favourite indie albums. The kids were, as yet, oblivious to the gentle smoulder of past love Kim was enthusiastically fanning, hoping that any moment now it would combust into fully-fledged flames.

Stan's backpack was by the door and Gigi was still packing and repacking her small suitcase, never sure which books to take and which pencil case had the felt pens which were up to the job of creating a catwalk-worthy gown design – as was her current obsession.

Finally ready, Gigi rolled her wheely bag through to the living room as if she was at airport departures, setting off to Paris fashion week. She looked her mum up and down.

"You're fancy," she said, with a tone which sounded like a blend of suspicion and disapproval.

"Yeah, you're right," Kim said, with a flamboyant exuberance. "I'm just so fancy. All the time."

Gigi laughed. "No you're not. You're usually in leggings and hoodies. And today you've got lipstick on. And your hair is straightened." Gigi's mouth opened as if some realisation swept through her being. "Are you looking fancy for dad?" Her eyes lit up. "Do you want to have more babies with dad?"

"Woah, woah, woah," Kim blurted, sitting upright on the slouchy sofa. "Slow down a bit, petal. Just because I've made a bit of effort, that does not mean there will be babies! Crikey."

"But you like him?" Gigi asked, trying to stifle pure joy.

Kim shrugged. "I just felt like putting on a nice top. Is that so bad? Maybe I have plans for after he picks you up."

"Do you?"

Damn. Outsmarted by a seven-year-old again.

Thinking quickly, Kim trotted out a lie. "I'm going to Brydie's for coffee."

"You normally do that without all the makeup," Gigi continued.

"OK, that's enough, Miss Marple," Kim said, getting to her feet to take her finished coffee cup through to the kitchen.

"Who's Miss Marple?"

Kim flashed her daughter an exasperated glance. "So many questions."

Forty minutes passed and still no sign of Rick. Stan was oblivious, lying on his bed watching a random video of toys being unboxed on his tablet. Gigi had taken to sitting on the footstool, looking out the living room window, propping her chin up with one hand, clutching her suitcase handle with the other.

It was a pretty sad sight, Kim thought, as she stood behind her, arms folded, also looking out the window.

Something snapped in Kim's mind and she marched into the hallway, bellowing, "Right! Grab your stuff kids, we're going to dad's!"

The three of them – one on a frustration-powered mission, one clutching a suitcase with a sorrowful expression and the other singing the theme tune to Bing – piled into Kim's rusty old Fiesta and drove the five minutes it took to get the other side of the village to a small council estate where Rick was renting a room from a workmate.

She parked outside, right behind Rick's car – evidence he must be home.

Kim got out of the car with force and called backwards to the kids to wait in their seats. This was a solo job. She strutted down the path, head bent forward slightly in determination and rang the door bell. She added a couple of fist thuds on the door for effect, and also to let out some of her pent up tension.

The door opened to the sight of a woman, probably in

her early twenties, wearing a long T-shirt with bare legs and messy bed hair.

"Hiya," she croaked, clearly not long out of bed. "You alright?"

"Yeah, I'm alright," Kim replied urgently. "Where's Rick?"

"Oh, you must be the baby-momma," the woman replied with a misty grin. She wandered off down the hallway without a word, leaving Kim standing at the open door. Kim overheard her calling out: "Babe! That's your ex. I thought you were kidless today?"

Babe? What the hell? Kim's heartrate quickened as thoughts of panic whooshed around her skull. *Please don't say I've been an absolute idiot. Please say that's his housemate's overly friendly girlfriend. Babe.*

After a minute – which was a minute too long in Kim's opinion – Rick appeared at the door in a dark green dressing gown, bleary-eyed and confused.

"What the fuck, Rick?" she blurted out, unable to contain her fury. "Your children have been waiting an hour for you to pick them up. Clearly you've forgotten."

He stiffened as the realisation crept over him. "Shit. I'm so sorry."

He glanced behind him anxiously, then came out onto the doorstep and closed the door.

"Who was that?" Kim asked, pointing to the now-closed door. "A fling?"

"What's it to do with you?" he responded defensively. "I'm a grown-up. What I do on my own time shouldn't matter to you."

"This isn't *your own time*, Rick!" Kim responded, practically spitting out the words. "It's daddy o'clock now. This is your time with the kids."

There was silence as Rick glanced at the two pairs of eyes peering over from inside the car.

"Nice move," he said, sarcastically. "Humiliate me in front of them."

"You've humiliated yourself, Rick. Don't pin that on me."

The door opened and the young woman eyed Kim suspiciously before placing a hand on Rick's shoulder and asking: "Everything alright babe? Need a hand?"

Kim's face stiffened with anger.

In a flustered haze, Rick shooed the woman back inside and turned to Kim, his face a mixture of embarrassment and defiance.

"So, I guess you're seeing someone," Kim said, able to keep her voice low and measured, despite the pounding heartrate and rushing chemicals inside her.

"We never said we'd go exclusive yet," he said, defensively. "I know what you're like and knew you'd probably drop me again because I'm not good enough for you."

Kim was stunned.

She glanced at the ground, formulating her tangled thoughts into a clear thread she could comprehend. "Let me get this straight," she eventually said. "You kept a sidepiece going, in case it didn't work out with me... because you knew you couldn't hold your shit together long enough to prove we could do this?"

Rick folded his arms and bit his lip in frustration, offering no reply.

"Oh my god," Kim cried, throwing her hands up in surrender. "I don't know what I was thinking. Of course this was never going to work. You're....an idiot. A selfish, big kid with no backbone. Fuck. You."

She turned around to walk towards the car, aware of keeping her composure so the kids wouldn't see how upset she was. Without turning back, she called out: "You can take the kids tomorrow instead...when you're more competent."

She felt a pang of disgust in her stomach at the thought of her kids even being at his shag pad. Thank god they slept at his mum's and not there.

In the car, she took a deep breath and feigned humour. "Oh dear, we had a bit of a mix up," she said to the kids with a forced smile. "You'll go to daddy's another day. He's not well."

"I heard you getting cross," Gigi said, her glare fixed on Kim.

Kim stared straight ahead, her insides screaming. "Don't worry about that. We're still friends. I'm just a bit tired."

The drive home was excruciating, asking Stan about which toys were unboxed in the video he watched to lighten the mood in the car and to push back the fierce emotion which was threatening to pierce Kim's eyes to allow tears to gush forth. The rest of the afternoon was similarly anguishing. Kim hid in the bathroom sobbing off and on, between answering questions about what puppies eat and how rockets fly – her extent of knowledge on this was: "they use petrol, or diesel, or some sort of fuel. Go and ask Google, or Siri or whoever it is you ask."

She texted a mayday callout to Brydie, asking for some company that evening once the kids were bedded.

True to form, Brydie appeared on the doorstep with a bottle of pink gin and a cautious smile at 8pm.

"I wasn't going to drink," Kim said meekly, her bloodshot eyes a clear giveaway that she did not have her shit together.

Brydie took control and walked through to the kitchen to raid the cupboards for glasses and investigate the fridge for mixers. She squinted her face in disapproval to find the only suitable mixer of a can of red cola and said: "This will have to do. By the looks of things, these are emergency drinks." She placed a pillar-box red drink firmly in Kim's hand and led her through to the lounge to slump on the sofa together.

"What's happened?" Brydie asked, putting one hand on Kim's knee.

Kim put her drink on the side table and pulled out a long, stringy piece of loo roll from up her sleeve, like the lowest rate magician you could ever imagine, and began dabbing her eyes and nose whilst delivering the whole story in muffled words through tissue and between sobs.

"I'm so stupid. You can say it," Kim said, finally pausing to take a breath.

"I'm never going to say that," Brydie reassured, keeping full composure. "You had to try this to find out, I guess. I've been thinking about it all and I totally get how scary and lonely it must be sometimes, being the only adult in the house. I was trying to work out what you saw in Rick and I realised it was comfort – the familiarity of it all. You hoped he could do better. That's not your fault. Not at all."

Kim smiled, through her anguish. "And I really didn't mean those things I said about you having it easy. I know it's not all perfect for you."

Brydie shook her head. "Hey, don't worry about it. I do have a nice life. In fact, I've done loads and loads of thinking and I'm actually OK with just being a step mum. I've been looking around at people....like Ray, for example. She's amazing. She hasn't had kids. Yet, she gives out so much love. She IS love. You know what I mean?"

Kim nodded in agreement. "She's awesome. I want to get her round a beach fire and listen to more of her stories."

"And she wouldn't have done all those things if she'd followed a conventional path," Brydie added. "I'm realising there's more to this whole 'life' thing than just what we're expected to do."

They held out their glasses for a cheers and took a swig of their red cola pink gins.

Kim laughed. "This is actually rather lovely. Do you fancy some super posh nibbles to go with this top-rate cocktail? I have a tube of squeezy cheese we could deliver straight into the receptacles," she offered, pointing to her wide open mouth.

Brydie threw back her head and exclaimed: "Yes!! Please!! Squeeze it straight in my gob."

A few sips and a few squeezes of cheese later and Kim's tissue – or rather, strands of shredded tissue – were tucked back in her sleeve. Brydie was glad to see the end of that sorry, soggy white flag.

"Hey! I have some good news," Brydie said, sitting up and becoming very animated. "We raised just over seven hundred pounds last night!"

Kim shrieked and grabbed Brydie's hand to wave it about in celebration.

"We should do more charity events," Brydie added. "Now that we've built this little community, we should use it."

"Absolutely," Kim agreed.

"I have some other news," Brydie said, a little more straight-laced. "I've applied for a job at the dolphin spotting centre."

"No way," Kim said, sitting up straight.

"All the organising for the solstice dook gave me a bit of a confidence boost," Brydie continued. "I hate to sound big-headed…but I'll brag anyway… I think I was damned good at pulling things together, and I absolutely loved it."

"This is amazing," Kim said, her eyes wide with joy.

"The job is organising displays and co-ordinating tours and school trips and such. And I *really* want it."

The evening had transformed from one of tears and trauma to excitement and sharing in mutual admiration – just as it always did when these two women got together.

Talk turned to their new hobby in the water and before long they were bent double in laughter.

"Remember last week when I dove right under and you said you were too scared to put your head right under?" Brydie asked, barely able to get the words out through laughter. "The next thing I see is you diving right in, just this blonde hair floating past me like a wig on the surface and I'm thinking 'wow, well done Kim, you actually did it'… and then you appeared, completely drenched and shocked saying the wave had knocked you over by accident."

Kim was reaching back in her sleeve for the dreaded straggly strand of tissue to wipe her tears of laughter as she nodded in agreement. "Yes," she bleated. "I was so confused when I eventually surfaced and you were giving me a round of applause and smiling at me."

Brydie sighed. "It was such a disappointment to learn you just fell over."

"I have an idea…." Kim said, pausing to think it through. "OK. I'm just going to say it. Feel free to say no if it's stupid, but I think we should get matching tattoos of something like a wave, or a fish...something to do with the sea."

Brydie laughed. "You know what? You're on. I'm feeling a little tattooey. A bit bold."

They began plotting and planning their ink outing and by the time they'd downed the last of the red drink and hugged a few hundred times – or so it seemed – Kim's soul was so much brighter as she waved Brydie off down the street. Life was back in balance. As she checked on her sleeping children in their shared bedroom, breathing heavily under their plump covers, she smiled in the realisation that she was no worse off than she had been a few weeks ago, before the whole Rick resurgence. She still had this cosy home, she had her job, her health, her best friend and a new 'cocktail' under her belt. However, she vowed never to recommend a red cola and pink gin to anyone, she was way too classy for that. That desperate concoction could stay between friends.

CHAPTER 26 – MARTHA

Sporting blue latex gloves with a toilet brush in hand, Martha was busy cleaning her ninth toilet of the shift when her mind began to wander to environmental issues. It bothered her that she had to use a new pair of latex gloves between every task. She had visions of an enormous hill of discarded gloves at the end of every day in this hospital. Humans make a lot of mess. And then she would remind herself that vulnerable patients could get very ill, or even die, if she didn't throw away gloves between tasks. The cross-contamination between toilet to sink, or toilet to patient's water jug could be deadly. She sighed at the ecological conundrum. She had no choice but to continue churning through the rubber and adding to the pile of waste.

Her thoughts were interrupted as someone rushed into the small space, taking up what little room there was behind Martha's back.

"I'll be finished in a minute," she said without looking up, assuming it was a patient ready to soil her glistening loo.

"Martha, it's Ron," came the rushed reply of her supervisor.

She stood up from her bent position, still clutching the toilet brush. Her eyes were wide with worry.

"He's in A&E," her supervisor continued. "They phoned up to the ward and asked for you. I'll get someone else to come and take over. You'd better go down there."

Martha didn't say a word. She dropped the brush back

in its pot, yanked off the gloves and tossed them straight in the freshly changed bin, washed her hands with wild urgency and power-walked through the ward, hands still dripping wet.

"Hi Martha, did you have a nice weekend?" Bill, the porter, asked as she passed.

She couldn't respond. She was fixated on her route to Ron. Her mind was busy with worry. Voices and sights around her were blurred as if she was passing by on a speeding train. *It's probably just a cut from a tool*, she thought, hopefully. *He's always under a boat with tools. And he's a clumsy oaf. That's what it'll be.* But her pounding heartbeat revealed the truth about her fear. She was merely pretending to rationalise the situation.

She reached A&E and met her cleaning colleague Anne who said, gently: "He's in cubicle five. They know you're coming." Anne looked grim. This wasn't a good sign.

Martha reached cubicle five, her heart now racing and her facial features stiff like stone in a panicked formation.

"Mrs Scott?" the doctor in blue scrubs queried.

Martha nodded. Her eyes fell on the sight of her husband lying on a bed, oxygen mask covering half his face and a heart monitor beeping repetitively next to him. Panic set in. She began gasping air desperately, unable to ask any questions.

The doctor sat in a plastic chair and gestured for Martha to sit in the opposite chair. In calm tones, she began explaining that Ron had collapsed at work and the ambulance crew had to restart his heart with a defibrillator.

Martha began sobbing. "I knew there was something up," she confessed. "I told him weeks ago to go for a check-up. I should have booked it myself."

The doctor sympathised. "Hey, don't do that to yourself. He's in really good hands now. We've scanned him and we're putting him through for a coronary angioplasty tomorrow morning. That means his artery will be fitted with a stent to keep it open and maintain blood flow to the heart. The surgeon will be in later to explain everything to you, OK?"

Martha nodded. She was in complete shock. She had no words. "Is he…awake?" Martha asked weakly.

The doctor smiled supportively, "he'll be in and out of consciousness, but yes, you can talk to him and let him know you're here. He needs lots of rest, but he'll be glad to hear you. He was saying your name over and over when he arrived."

Tears spilled over the threshold of Martha's eyelids and soaked her pale cheeks as she rose from the chair to Ron's bedside. She took his hand gently in hers and bent over the bed slightly, saying: "Oh Ron. I'm here."

He struggled to open his eyes and tried to say the word Martha, but with the oxygen mask, and a dry mouth it came out as a hissing croak.

"It's OK," she said in a whisper. "Don't try to talk. The doctor says you're getting surgery and you'll be better. Your heart stopped, Ron. Bloody hell." Her voice faltered as emotion washed over her. "I could have lost you. You're not allowed to go yet."

His eyes were locked on hers, a desperate gratitude flowing between their gaze.

Martha stroked his forehead and told him to rest. She was going to phone her mother to explain she wouldn't be popping round later on and she'd be back.

Martha left A&E to go home for some of Ron's things and to change out of her turquoise domestic uniform, which by now felt suffocating and restrictive with hospital grimness. The plan had been that Ron would be picking her up that night, so she called a taxi to take her home. The driver could sense – due to Martha's wide-eyed, traumatised face – it wasn't one of those journeys that called for polite chat, which she was extremely grateful for.

Back at the house, she poured a cup of hot tea and sat in silence at the kitchen table, allowing her mind to process the event and try to settle in to the fact that Ron was being constantly monitored at the hospital, and that should anything happen, they knew what to do.

When she eventually felt strong enough to do so, she called her mum, unsure what to expect, as there was always something weird going on in the household these days. A week ago the phone kept ringing out, causing Martha to panic with all sorts of sordid visions of death or delirium. It turned out – after she rushed round there – that the phone was in the freezer. Panic averted.

"Hello?" her mother answered, sounding flustered.

"Hi, Mum, it's me," Martha said, wearily.

"Good. I need your help!"

"What? Why?"

"Your father's missing."

Martha bent her head forward in anguish and hit her mobile phone off her forehead several times in frustration. *Not now. Please not now.* Her headbutting had selected a wordsearch app by accident. "Are you still there mum?" she asked urgently, pulling it up to her ear again.

Her mother cut across her and launched straight into a frantic explanation. "He packed his lunch and said he was going for a ramble, like he always used to do. I haven't seen him since eleven o'clock this morning. It's now six, for goodness sake. He hasn't even had his afternoon tea and biscuits. I've got the carer driving around looking for him. Would you send Ron out? Ron knows all the walking routes."

"Ron's in hospital," Martha uttered, knowing there would be no point explaining the full story right now, while her mother was in crisis mode. "I'll go out in the car."

"Thank you!" her mother said and hung up abruptly.

"Aaargrrgghh!" Martha let out a guttural scream and swept the placemats off the table with her forearm. "Why does it have to today dad loses his final marble?" She buried her face in her hands for a moment, then pulled herself together with a huge deep intake of breath, went through to the bedroom to pull on a pair of jogging bottoms and a sweatshirt that said "fun times" – which made Martha roll her eyes – and grabbed her car keys.

When she turned the key in the ignition, music blasted on at high volume. It was the Stereophonics – Ron's music. Loud, as always. Martha stabbed at the stereo power button until it ceased all noise. She began sobbing quietly as she pulled out of the drive, the stress of the day weighing heavily on her, but aware she had no choice but to power on.

She drove up to the woods and parked at the clearing. This had always been a favourite spot of his when she was a kid. She got out and called into trees: "Dad?" A silent minute later, she called out again, but even louder this time: "Dad?!"

She weighed up her choices – walk into the woods, which could be a total waste of time, or keep driving along the coast looking for him on the footpath. How the hell would she know which option to take? She dialled the carer's number.

"Hi Martha," Dana said warmly. "The police are with me just now. And the local walking group are heading out along the well-known paths."

Martha was still sobbing but now it became more urgent. "Thank you, Dana. Thank you. I can't cope with this right now. Ron had a heart attack. He's in hospital."

"Oh my," Dana responded in shock. "We'll find your dad. You just concentrate on Ron."

"Mum and dad can't go on like this," Martha said through tumbling anguish, her voice giving in to the struggle. "They need round the clock care, don't they?"

"Yes," Dana agreed, without a moment of hesitation. "I've been speaking to the social worker. We can start looking into options now. We'll get together with you and go over it all. But yes, it's time. They're not safe on their own."

Later that night, as Martha sat by Ron's hospital bed, snoozing in an armchair, refusing to go home to bed, she was awoken by the vibrating of a text message. It was Dana: "Found ur dad. He was halfway to Dooniemoss. Blisters on his feet and freezing, but otherwise OK. Looking into temporary sheltered accommodation, til you make some decisions."

Martha sighed with relief. She looked at Ron, checking that everything still looked the same as before she'd shut her eyes. The heart monitor was still beeping at the same measured rate. He was still sleeping. All was OK. It was 1am. She gave in. It would be acceptable to go home to bed, just for a bit. As long as she was here in the morning before the big operation.

CHAPTER 27 – RAY

Sunlight snuck in through the edges of the curtains in Ray's boudoir. She always called it a boudoir. Never a bedroom.

It was only 6am, but her mind was sharp, despite the measures of neat rum the night before. There was no point in trying to get any more sleep, she decided. She glanced over at Mike, who was deep in slumber next to her. It was the first time he'd stayed over, and to Ray's surprise there was nothing weird about waking up next to him. It felt completely natural. His mouth hung open slightly as he breathed in and out with a gentle rasping sound. She gently rolled over and sat up slowly so as not to disturb him. She was damned if we she was going to change her regular routine for a man. The beach was calling her.

She threw on a kaftan and leggings, slipped into some sandals, grabbed her bag with all her meditating 'accessories' and snuck out.

As she pulled the front door firmly closed, hearing the click which signalled security, she grinned with satisfaction, remembering the day Mike fixed it.

She walked the short distance to the sandy bay, a soft smile decorating her face and cool sea air filling her lungs with the freshness of a new day.

She found a spot on the pale, yellow sand and rolled out her little rug to sit on.

Crossed legged, with hands resting on her thighs, she closed her eyes and began listening to the gulls crying and the waves swishing in and out. A giggle tugged at her throat as she got flashbacks of the night before. Captain Lamebeard striking a pose in her living room, holding a bottle of rum in the air like a weapon. They had decided they were both pirates in a past life and had spent an hour or so creating a back story and character names for who they believed they had been. Mike was Lamebeard, on account of the fact he was such a gentle soul he could never have maimed and harmed enemies. He would have tried to reason with them, and end up with several scars in the process. Ray's character was called Rebel Tooth Ray, as she had a couple of gold teeth thanks to partying too hard in her twenties and thirties. The couple had laughed so hard during their pirate chat she noticed streaks of mascara under her eyes later on when she was getting ready for bed. It had been wonderful to be so carefree into the small hours – like time and age didn't exist.

She opened her eyes. Her mind was too full of hilarity and visions of Mike for any form of peaceful meditation. She smiled as she looked across the water to the horizon, letting the serenity of the sight mingle with her giddy joy.

She glanced at the bag. Normally, this might be the time for a little smoke, or a nibble of 'special' cake, but she really didn't feel like it, much to her surprise. In fact, she realised, it had been a week since she'd last delved into her supply. She had a lightness in her soul that surpassed any feelings she could get from smoking. She left the bag untouched on the sand and took in some deep breaths, noticing the comforting aroma of seaweed in the air. It wasn't exactly a beautiful smell. In fact, Ray often thought seaweed smelled a bit farty. But it was the familiarity of it and what it represented that she enjoyed.

After ten minutes sitting on her little rug, she decided

her soul was cleansed enough and she packed her things away to head for home. She had plans for later that day. Martha had gone off the radar and Ray wanted to check in on her absent swim buddy.

A few hours later, after sending Mike packing, politely of course, Ray was armed with a wicker basket full of flowers and honey for Martha and a little cloth bag containing a smooth, polished piece of bloodstone for Ron. She had chosen that particular stone because of its healing properties for recovering from illness.

When she arrived at Martha's house, Ray noticed how neat the front garden was. It was a modest semi-detached bungalow with a trimmed front lawn and blooming flower beds running along the walls under the windows. All very well cared for.

She rang the bell and waited. A few moments later, Martha opened the door and the shock of seeing Ray immediately showed on her face.

Martha looked pale, tired...unlike her usual self.

"Oh wow, Ray," Martha gushed, still looking taken aback. "What can I do for you?"

"I just wanted to check in on you," Ray said warmly. "It's been a few weeks since you last dooked and we're missing you. We heard what happened, so...if there's anything you need..."

Tears formed in Martha's eyes as her face crumpled in emotion. "Come in," she whispered and moved aside to let Ray in and gestured towards the kitchen.

Ray glanced around as she walked through the hallway. Everything was neat and tidy. There were only a few picture frames on the walls, in complete contrast to Ray's opulent, jam-packed art gallery walls. The frames contained family photos of graduations and a group photo at what must have been a significant wedding anniversary with Martha and Ron cutting a cake, fairly recently, their family all gathered around them.

"You have a lovely home," Ray said as she took a seat at the kitchen table and watched Martha fill the kettle. "So tidy."

Martha laughed. "It's probably a bit boring compared to your house."

"Not at all," Ray insisted. "People's homes are like exhibitions of what's important to them. Yours is lovely. It's all family and order."

Eventually, when two cups of tea were brewed, Martha sat at the kitchen table, a little on edge.

"How have things been?" Ray asked with confident ease, letting Martha know she could be real with her.

Martha sighed and looked into her cup. "It's been horrendous really," she said, her brow creasing. "I don't feel I can leave Ron at all, in case…it happens again. I just…I keep going over in my head what it would have been like if they couldn't revive him. I don't know how I would have coped." She allowed the tears to break free and roll down her cheeks.

Ray put a hand over Martha's hand. "Of course you're processing it all. That's natural."

Martha sniffed. "I feel so guilty that I didn't push him to go to the doctor when he started feeling unwell."

"Hey," Ray interjected softly. "You're giving yourself such a hard time. Once you've allowed yourself to have all these feelings, you need to start reminding yourself that they *did* resuscitate him, he *is* here and you've been given this chance to move on and live life together."

There was silence while Martha nodded and took a sip of tea. "I suppose it's scared me. I don't want him to go anywhere or do anything that might put strain on his heart."

Ray asked: "Did the doctors tell you what he should be able to do?"

Martha nodded. "They said, with the stent in, his heart is as strong as ever. He can start getting back to normal over the next few weeks, slowly."

Ray smiled. "That's great." Then sensing there was more, she asked: "Are you struggling to accept that?"

Martha shrugged. "I just don't want to go through that again. Or worse. It's also frightened me about my own health. We share the same diet, the same lifestyle, give or take a bit of golf, which I won't touch. What if my heart can't take much activity?"

Ray suddenly had a realisation. "Is this why you've stopped swimming?"

"Yes," Martha admitted. "The cold water is so shocking, what if my heart can't take it? I'm no spring chicken. I don't want to cause a fuss by collapsing in the freezing cold water."

Ray, stroked her lips as she pondered those words for a moment. "OK," she eventually said. "I hear you. That's totally understandable. However...before Ron's... trauma... you had no issues in the sea, am I right?"

Martha nodded in agreement.

"And you've had no signs of anything that tells you it's bad for your health, no?" Ray continued.

"No," Martha said meekly.

"In fact, you said it helped ease your achy hips, yeah?" Ray asked.

Again, Martha nodded.

"I can't see any reason why you can't still enjoy the sea. You loved it so much. Even just the social benefits are amazing, aren't they? Think how much we laugh and how great we feel when we get out. We're positively buzzing. I'm no spring chicken either. Age doesn't matter. In fact, the older I get, the more I think 'to hell with it' and just embrace shit. Besides, you're safe with us. Brydie has every little eventuality covered, the adorable little nerd that she is."

Martha smiled through tears and took Ray's hand in hers.

"I'm not trying to force you into dooking again, it's completely up to you," Ray added. "But it would be a shame to see that bright, confident woman I got to know in the sea, retreat inside herself." Ray took a sip of tea, allowing her words to settle in Martha's mind, before saying: "There's a swim on tomorrow at eleven if you can manage it. And if not, we'll still be there next week. And the week after."

Martha grinned. "I'll think about it. Even Ron has been telling me to get back in the sea. It's only me who's put everything off. He's desperate to get back to normal."

"See? He's a good lad," Ray said with a smile. "He doesn't want this to hold either of you back. In other news, we've seen a little bit less of Brydie too. She got the job!"

Martha gasped. "Good for her. She'll be brilliant at the dolphin centre. She's so driven."

Ray nodded in agreement and added: "She's really come out of her shell since we met her, hasn't she? We did an early evening swim yesterday so she could still fit one in. Wouldn't be the same without her."

Ray took one last gulp of tea and took to her feet and lifted the gifts out of her basket ready to take it home. "You take care," she said, giving Martha a tight hug and secretly sending positive affirmations from her mind to

Martha's.

As she stepped out onto the shingle garden path, she turned around and said with a wink, "maybe see you tomorrow, beautiful."

Martha nodded with an electric smile.

CHAPTER 28 – HOT STUFF

"This'll be a really nice change," Kim said, gazing out the passenger window as Brydie drove them to Findhoun, a fifteen-minute car ride along the coast. "Thanks for remembering my birthday."

Brydie grinned. "Hey, how could I let your special day go by without forcing you to dunk your ass in that wild October sea? It's going to be a rough one today."

Kim sighed. "Is this your version of Birthday bumps? Instead of kneeing me in the behind, you're going to let the waves do it for you?"

Brydie laughed. "Exactly!"

They parked up at the beach carpark and carried their heavy swim bags, laden with spare woolly hats and flasks full of hot drinks, up the grassy hill to a platform which gave way to smart wooden steps leading to the stoney beach. Findhoun beach is so different to Brogie's equivalent. For a start, Findhoun is always busier. It's a destination beach with cafes and boat trips setting off from its spectacular bay at one side and money thrown at its other beach, with its colourful modern beach huts, which sell for tens of thousands of pounds, and new timber work to make the area more accessible. The village is also home to a world famous foundation where spiritual folk from all over the world flock for workshops, meditations and to be part of the independent eco settlement. If Findhoun and Brogie were relatives, Findhoun would be the classy cousin who got all the top notch Christmas gifts, was popular at school and had parents who grew their own vegetables and practiced daily meditation. Brogie Bay was the rugged, but kind-hearted kid in the family – not quite as refined, but happy in its own skin.

Standing at the top of the beach steps, Brydie and Kim glanced along the coastline to see Brogie sitting proudly at the other end of this curve of coast which linked the two villages. The large white, malt factory loomed over the village streets, making it impossible to forget the contrast between holiday haven Findhoun and hard-working down to earth Brogie.

Kim gasped to see a collection of changing robe-clad women waving in her direction. "What are they doing here?" she cried, turning to Brydie in amazement?

The Dookers began walking over, against a backdrop of dark, moody ocean, sporting woolly bobble hats in a variety of colours, smiles yanking at their expressions excitedly. Kim let out a laugh as she noticed they were desperately trying to hold on to metallic party cones perching precariously on top of their winter hats.

Martha blew a little plastic party horn while Ray and Lisa yelled "Happy birthday" over the thundering noise of the intimidating waves.

Kim threw her hands to her mouth in shock as tears formed in her eyes. "Did you organise this?" she asked, turning to Brydie.

"Team effort," Brydie replied, clearly brimming with joy. "And look." She turned her friend by the shoulders and pointed out a little black horse box about fifty metres away. "We're going there."

"What the…?" Kim was bemused.

The group were now surrounding the Birthday girl,

with Martha busying herself attaching a hat to Kim's head. There were excited murmurings all around as Kim asked what on earth they were going to be doing in a horse trailer.

"Wait and see," said Ray, with absolute mischief in her eyes.

They walked closer and, through squinted eyes, Kim made out the word 'sauna'. The horse box had been converted by a local company into a sauna for beach-dwellers. Perfect on a crisp autumnal day.

Kim's face radiated excitement as she threw off her cosy changing robe and declared "Time to warm my cockles!"

"Before freezing them off," Lisa added with a grin.

The group kicked off their surf boots and entered the tiny wooden door. Inside the trailer was a stunning scene of fresh pine seating, an enormous window looking out onto the churning ocean and a little stove generating dry heat. The calming scent of warm wood surrounded the Dookers as they lay towels out to protect their naked flesh from the searing surface.

Kim exhaled in pleasure. "This is amazing. Thank you, guys. I can't believe I'm sitting here, hot as hell, while looking out at that moody grey sky and those enormous waves. Are we really going to get in there?"

"We must," said Ray, oozing delight. "Even if we only go in thigh deep, to get the cooling spray on us."

Chat turned to everyone's weekend plans and the promise of cosy TV nights, homemade feasts and stiff drinks.

"Right, I'm either going to pass out with the heat, or I need to get in that sea," Brydie declared, puffing and fanning her face with her hands.

"Good call," Kim responded. "I think my necklace is burning my skin it's so hot in here."

One by one, the pink, bug-eyed women stumbled out the door and down the little wooden ramp, gasping for cool air.

"Woah," Lisa bellowed. "Look at our red lobster thighs. They're even more red than usual. Do you think going from one temperature extreme to the other will give me varicose veins?"

She looked around for answers. Martha shrugged.

Brydie responded with an air of authority: "It's supposed to be really good for circulation – the dilating and constricting of blood vessels going between the two extremes."

"Ooh, look who's been researching again," Kim retorted, throwing a loving wink Brydie's way.

The cold air pricked like pins against the women's naked flesh as they trotted down the sand and pebble slope towards the roaring water.

Ray let out the first scream as fresh sea foam slapped her hips. "Holy crap that's cold!"

There were shrieks of laughter melting into shrieks of pain all around. It was a sordid soundtrack, which had dog walkers wrapped up in coats stopping in their tracks, some laughing, some scratching their heads in wonder. It was quite a sight, and quite a sound.

An enormous peak of dark water suddenly lurched up, rolling fast towards the Dookers. It's white head of foam loomed high. Like an angry goddess, it leapt towards them powerfully.

Screams struck out as women fell about in the force of the wave.

Kim was the last to surface, laughing ecstatically, hair

dripping wet. "Wow. The current pulled my feet out from under me!" she shouted to the others. "I've never felt it so strong."

"I'm not keen on big waves," Lisa admitted and found a comfortable spot where the water level just grazed her thighs.

Martha surprised the others by leaping head on into the body of a tall wave, allowing it to engulf her. When she eventually emerged, soggy and rubbing her eyes, she shouted: "What's it they say!? Go big or go home!"

"Martha! Your boob is hanging out!" Brydie warned, with a giggle.

"Oh my!" Martha declared, popping it back inside her swimsuit. "Well, now I can finally say I've skinny-dipped...almost!"

The group trudged back to the sauna to warm up once more. More chat and giggles could be heard from outside the hut as they put the world to rights, before re-emerging into the brisk autumnal air to embrace the sea again.

The waves were not in a peaceful mood. The sheer force each wave exerted on the shins of the Dookers made them decide not to risk going in any deeper.

There were large boulders at the water's edge. "Why don't we just sit on those rocks, like mermaids?" Kim suggested. "We'll still feel the effect of the cool sea spray."

One by one they each found a boulder suitable for perching on and got comfy, just in time for an enormous gush of tide to rip roar towards them, knocking Ray, Lisa and Brydie off their rocks.

The drenched trio, sat up on the pebbly sand, laughing.

"That wasn't particularly glamorous!" Ray announced, pulling a strand of seaweed from her head.

"It's so powerful today," Martha said, in awe as she stared out at the rolling waves stampeding towards the women.

The women were now all standing, bubbles of seafoam popping and hissing noisily around their ankles as the aftermath of the wave slid back down the sand to the main body of water.

They put their arms around each other, forming a team line-up of smiling, breathless friends, facing the ruthless Moray Firth.

CHAPTER 29 – LISA

T he past few weeks had tumbled by quickly for Lisa, a blend of DIY and dooking. The house was still so far away from where she and Heather wanted it to be, but it had oodles more style and between them they'd nursed wooden doors and ornate features back to their former glory. It was...better.

She was eating a cheese toastie and salad for lunch at the kitchen island when Heather entered the room in a long, black evening gown with what looked like moth-eaten holes and shredded sleeves. Her long black hair was down for a change and straightened and she had dark crimson lips and charcoal, smudged eye make-up plunging her chocolate brown pupils into the shadows. It was startling for Lisa to see her wife, who normally never touched a drop of make-up, be so extravagant. She coughed on a piece of bread with the shock and had to take a big swig of water to force it down. "What the...."

Heather placed her hands on her hips dramatically and oozed in a deep voice: "I can't host my woman's Halloween night without making a bit of effort." She threw back her head and let out a forced cackle.

Lisa's face was alive with amusement. "Wow," was all she could say as she took in the sight from head to toe. "You look really hot as a... what are you?"

"I'm the original owner of this mansion," Heather replied with conviction, eyeing Lisa intensely – attempting to summon her character fully. "I died hundreds of years ago...and every Halloween I return to remind the present owners that THIS IS MY HOUSE!" She attempted an evil bellowing voice, which only made Lisa laugh even more.

"Awesome," Lisa said with a grin. "What the hell am I going to wear? I was just going to chuck on last year's bat wings headband, but after seeing this…"

Heather strutted over to the kettle to fill it, swishing her hair and throwing a nasty look at Lisa as she moved. Then, breaking character ever so suddenly, she said: "This house is going to be the perfect setting for your party. I can't wait. I'll have it all lit by candles in the hallway in time for you getting back from the swim and I'll play creepy organ music while you all come in."

"On your organ?" Lisa asked sarcastically.

"Yeah, I've been secretly taking lessons behind your back and I bought a huge pipe organ off eBay," Heather retorted, before adding: "On the Bluetooth speakers, silly."

Lisa abandoned her lunch to give her wife a hug and pulled back to look her in the eyes and say: "Thank you for all this. I'm really excited now. I was a bit nervous about asking everyone from the group to come up here, but it's going to be fun. You'll get to know them better too."

Heather's smile widened, flashing white teeth between her darkly painted lips. "You deserve this honey. It's about time we had a bloody party. Especially before I start sanding the floors. I don't care if we make a mess tonight because the floors are still gross."

Lisa squeezed Heather's waist in the fitted dress. "You should wear stuff like this more often."

Heather rolled her eyes. "Me and dresses don't get together very often. Enjoy this while it lasts, baby."

Clara's trainers thudded down the creaking stairs and

into the kitchen, and as her eyes fell on Heather she raised her eyebrows and laughed. "Okaaay," she said under her breath, shaking her head, grabbed a banana from the counter and left the room.

"Love you Clara!" Heather shouted after her in a joking tone. "Shall I come and do your make-up next?"

"No thank you!" Clara called as she ascended the stairs, before adding a cheery "Love you too."

Lisa and Heather smiled at each other before Lisa whispered: "She's definitely turned a corner. She's a lot happier since she started hanging out with Rebecca. She hasn't rolled her eyes in weeks."

"And that's saying something for a fifteen-year-old," Heather added. "Let's take that win and run with it. Anyway, come on, let's get you sorted with something to wear tonight."

Heather pulled Lisa by the hand towards the stairs.

"Remember I have to wear it with a swimsuit to begin with," Lisa said. "It's fancy dress dook, *then* the party, so nothing complicated please."

A few hours later, decked out in red face paint and devil horns, Lisa had on a red swimsuit and her black changing robe and surf boots. "I hope the red paint doesn't wash off in the sea," she said almost pleadingly, as she threw her bag over her shoulder to leave.

The sun was long gone and the night sky enveloped the village like a black velvet blanket. As she pulled up at the slipway in her car, she gasped to see the grim reaper with a glowing lantern. The reaper pulled its hood backwards to reveal Martha's cheery face as she gave Lisa a wave then pulled the hood back up to change demeanour instantly.

Brydie's face was concealed in zombie make-up, her hair was teased into a messy nest, she wore a ripped T-shirt that said 'lifeguard' on it and clutched a red, plastic swim float under one arm. "I'm a zombie lifeguard," she called out triumphantly. "I actually wore this to work today. Really scared a bunch of nursery kids on a dolphin spotting field trip. Oops."

Kim turned to greet Lisa, saying, "ah, it's the devil. I wondered when you'd appear." Kim was wearing a green, metallic dress with shells glued onto it, a pale blue wavy wig and glittering gems adhered across her forehead and brows. "I'm a sea witch," she said, matter-of-factly. "No-one seems to get it. Brydie thought I was a drag queen, which admittedly would have been cool, but I'm a sea witch."

"I love all your costumes," Lisa enthused.

Brydie strapped on a head torch, which shone directly into Kim's face like a spotlight manned by an overenthusiastic trainee at a theatre. "Argh, Bry, get that out of my eyes," she groaned.

"Sorry," the zombie lifeguard said, grimacing. "Safety first, we need to be able to see in the water, so I've brought a couple of these, if anyone else wants one."

"Aim it downwards, please," Kim said, fiddling with Brydie's torch to make it more friendly and less aggressive to onlookers.

"It's freezing tonight," Martha said, looking out into the darkness. You could no longer see over to the bay or out to the horizon. "There's been a definite drop in water temperature over the past two weeks hasn't there?"

"Yeah, it's going to get worse over the next few months, until about May really," Brydie responded. "We're up for it though, aren't we?"

"Oh yes!" Martha exclaimed. "I need my dooks."

Kim pulled out a rubber duck from her cleavage.

"Ducky-thermometer-guy will tell us what the water temperature is tonight. At the moment he's saying my boobs are twenty-five degrees. Let's see what number he gives us in the water."

"We're just waiting for Ray and Mike," Martha said. "Ron's going to come and watch, then take some of us up to the party after."

"Oh, did you both get your tattoos?" Lisa asked, eyeing Brydie then Kim.

Kim laughed. "Yeah, we did. We've had to cover them in waterproof plastic for the dook, but you should be able to see them through it."

They both held out their wrists, revealing an ink drawing of the crest of a wave. "Nice," Lisa remarked, examining them closely.

Kim started to giggle. "Don't you think mine looks more like a witch's crooked finger than a wave? Brydie's came out perfectly crisp, but god knows what happened to mine."

Lisa grimaced. "I see what you mean. It's chunkier."

Brydie put her arm around Kim. "I'm sorry. I feel bad that mine is better than yours. We shouldn't have rushed and taken the first available artist we could find."

Kim smiled. "It's actually OK. It's my wonky wave. And it reminds me of us, so it's no bad thing. I'll be the wonky one in this relationship."

Brydie laughed and added: "We're all a little wonky."

"Talking of wonky, look at this pair," Kim added, pointing across the grass.

"Hey!" came a call in the darkness as Ray and Mike were walking over from her cottage. Ray was wearing a long white coat, smeared with dirt and blood stains and some steampunk goggles with a huge frizzy grey wig. Mike was her Frankenstine-eqsue creature with bolts on his neck and stitches across his forehead.

"Ray whipped out what looked like a taser, pressed it to Mike's neck and made it glow and buzz while he acted as though she was electrocuting him, flinching and jerking, wailing "I'm alive, I'm alive."

Brydie let out a whoop. "Amazing!"

"Trust those two, to pull out all the stops," Kim said, laughing at the sight.

In a nondescript thick accent, Ray bellowed: "My creation needs to get in the water to cool down from all this electricity. He's a bit scorched. And then he's all mine. I created him with extra special features, ladies," she held her hands apart, indicating length. "And I'm taking orders, so you can let me know your requirements."

Wicked giggling filtered through the group at the suggestion.

Lisa interjected: "Er, no thanks. Not my bag." The group erupted in laughter.

"Of course. We can discuss alternative models, my dear," Ray responded, rubbing her hands together creepily.

Ron appeared with the car. He couldn't help but laugh at the sight of the spooky dookers. Mike patted Ron on the back and said with genuine warmth: "Nice to see you, mate."

"I've brought this massive torch," Ron said. "I can shine it from up here if you want. And I'll take pictures. You all look crazy. You won't want to miss photos of this."

It was time to embrace the chilly water.

Ron held up his phone, taking video footage of the gang of ghouls as they stepped gingerly into the sea, the usual chorus of shrieks and yelps as their warm skin was bitten by the chill.

Kim held Ducky-thermometer-guy underwater, as if she was inflicting torture to get the intel from him. A minute later she let him resurface and announced to the group: "Eleven degrees!"

"That's not too bad," Martha said. "We've had worse."

Brydie jumped and screamed. "Something brushed past my leg!"

"It'll just be seaweed," Ray reassured. "We can't see a thing. Let's go with seaweed."

Mike lunged forward to enjoy some breaststroke swimming. With Ray as his motivator, he'd well and truly acclimatised to swimming without his wetsuit. He now understood the attraction and pure high of the tingle from cold water, although, he did have to invest in a pair of neoprene swim shorts to protect his privates. He had tried on several occasions to convince the female group members that men felt the cold more sensitively on their privates, but in the end the reinforced shorts took that issue out of the equation. He no longer squirmed in agony as his nether region hit the water.

Martha waved up to Ron, who was snapping photos happily. She had ditched her grim reaper cape on dry land but was still proudly clutching her scythe.

"Who'd have thought I'd be dressing up as the grim reaper after what happened to Ron a few months ago," she said, pulling an awkward grin. "He thinks it's funny."

"You have to laugh," Ray agreed. "That's what life is all about."

"I cast a spell of good fortune on all the Dookers," Kim suddenly announced, throwing her arms up and embracing her sea witch character.

Brydie joked: "Anyone need saving? Just don't let me

get too close to your flesh. I'm feeling a bit nibbly."

Ray threw her hands down in the water dramatically, causing an enormous splash and bellowed: "Happy Halloween," before delivering an impressive witch's cackle. The others joined in, splashing all around, some howling, some laughing wickedly at blood-curdling volume.

A small gang of children nearby, who were knocking on doors along the sea front trick or treating replied with their own screams of "Happy Halloween".

After ten minutes of bobbing up and down and light breaststroke circles to keep moving, the group gradually swam back towards the slip, all sighing and sharing how exhilarated they felt. There was something extra intoxicating about dooking in darkness.

After getting dried and dressed under their thick changing coats, the group piled into a few cars and made their way up the hill to Lisa's.

In Lisa's car, she listened as Kim and Brydie were admiring the tree-lined driveway and saying how fitting this was for Halloween.

"No offence, Lisa," Brydie said, "but I feel like this could easily be a haunted house or murder mystery event."

Lisa smiled. "None taken. It is a creepy-ass house."

"It's gorgeous," Kim oozed, as they got out of the car and she stared up at the turret, backlit by moonlight. She then shrieked as Heather thrust open the door and stared at her guests menacingly. As promised, organ music flowed out from the hallway, giving a perfectly uneasy welcome. Lisa smiled proudly.

"Enter..." Heather said, hauntingly and Brydie giggled nervously as she made her way up the entrance steps and held her hand out, saying, "I'm Brydie."

Heather remained in character and looked Brydie up and down with a sour edge of disapproval.

Lisa kissed Heather's cheek and said with great amusement: "You don't have to stay in character all night. You can be nice for a little while."

Heather's intense stare broke into a warm smile as she laughed and started kissing cheeks and welcoming the Dookers to their spooky abode. "There's Cocktails of the Damned in the lobby there, grab yourself a glass."

Lisa was gobsmacked. "You organised all this? Cocktails and everything?"

Heather grinned. "I've been busy while you've been in the sea. It's all ready."

Ron pulled up with his carload of Dookers and Lisa could hear enthusiastic chatter as they entered the tiled porch and saw the gothic sight of a few dozen flickering candles around a wallpaper table, which Heather had disguised with a crimson bedsheet and had placed a punch bowl on top with a ladle and dozens of goblets which had skeleton hands gripping them.

Lisa picked one up to examine it. "Where did these come from?" she asked in wonder.

Heather patted the side of her nose with her index finger. She was keeping an air of mystery about her organisation skills.

Lisa, still as red as the devil himself – or herself, who knows? – and sporting her horns, grabbed a goblet and filled it with crimson liquid.

Heather announced to the group: "It's gin, cranberry and Cointreau. Enjoy."

Lisa led the group through to the lounge, which to her surprise had been draped in black velvet sheeting. The sofas were unrecognisable. Fake cobwebs hung from the ornate lighting overhead. Heather had done her proud. She could barely keep her mouth closed as he looked around at all the ghastly details. Heather shot her a sly look of satisfaction as she ushered the guests through and fiddled with her phone to adjust the playlist.

Heather made her way to Ron, who was thus far plain in his jeans and T-shirt. She held out a bag of accessories and without needing any more prompting, he thrust his hand in and pulled out a headband with a bloody plastic axe on it and immediately put it on his head, causing Martha to laugh and plant a kiss on his cheek.

The doorbell rang and Lisa ran to let Doug in.

"It's Doug!" Brydie called, already two Cocktails of the Damned in, and high on party spirit. "Quick, Heather, where's your fancy dress bag?" she called out.

Doug was manhandled into a long, flowing rainbow wig – not very scary, but outrageous nonetheless. He took it like a champ and made his way to the cocktail table for some liquid courage.

Lisa took a moment to look around at her new friends all chatting and laughing in their lounge. Wigs here, fake weapons there, bad face paint in every direction. It was pure bliss. She felt like this was a moment to remember. It was a sign that they'd well and truly settled in the village. These were her people now.

Suddenly, the lights flickered on and off. Lisa's heart skipped. Was this a new problem with the house she hadn't noticed before? Dodgy wiring. Another expense to pay for.

But when Clara and her new friend Rebecca appeared in the doorway dressed as eerie twins in blue dresses with braided pigtails and dead-eyed expressions, she felt relief flush through her. They had been flicking the lights on and off for effect. Then she felt surprise and awe at the fact that Clara was joining in. The two girls walked slowly through the room, staring straight ahead as if they had no souls, no feelings. It was effectively weird. They wandered to the other side of the room where another door led out to the hallway and very cleverly Clara hit the light switch again, plunging the Dookers and their partners into darkness for another few seconds as they left.

Lisa and Heather looked at each other, stunned.

"Wow," Heather mouthed silently and Lisa shrugged in amazement.

Clara and Rebecca passed the doorway again as they walked through the lobby and she gave her mum a mischievous thumbs up. Lisa laughed and blew Clara a kiss. It felt good to see her daughter socialise and be part of something they had planned as a household. She noticed Ray dashing out to the hallway to give Clara a big hug and Clara's face lit up as they chatted briefly.

The night wore on, as Heather invented more random cocktails.

At one point, everyone gathered round as an audience while Brydie, Kim and Ray acted out the song Stay by the Shakespeare Sisters with Brydie draped across three dining chairs, playing dead, Kim singing the main part and then Ray entering as the intensely gothic 'sister' for the creepy part of the song. Their onlookers gave love as if it was the greatest show they'd seen.

Eventually, it was time to wind down as energy levels were running low and enough cocktails to sink a ship had been consumed.

On the concrete steps, Martha turned to wave at Lisa and Heather, who were standing in the porch, arm in arm, waving their guests goodbye.

"I love you both," Martha called, blowing exaggerated kisses. She turned to find Ron and head for their car, but she lost her footing on the bottom step and tumbled head first into a bush by the bay window.

Kim was in hysterics. "I'll help her up!"

Kim reached down to give her friend a helping hand up, but she underestimated Martha's strength and instead got yanked down into the bush beside her.

Brydie stood, hand over her mouth, laughing at the pair. "I'm not going to attempt a rescue mission," she said. "I'd end up in there with you."

Instead, the two women were left to roll themselves out of the dense evergreen bush onto the shingle driveway and then slowly up onto their knees, both struggling with laughter. Ron looked on, his hand on his forehead in dismay, but with a smile tugging at his lips. It was quite the sight to behold – the grim reaper and a sea witch rolling about on the ground.

Eventually, all cars left the driveway and the house fell quiet.

Lisa and Heather enthused about what a great night it had been as they tucked into a leftover bowl of crisps with ravenous hunger. This had definitely been a night for the Dookers to remember.

CHAPTER 30 – HO, HO, HOLY SHIT, THAT'S COLD

Twenty-fourth of December. Every Christmas Eve leading up to this point in their lives, the Brogie Bay Dookers had spent this day fixated on last-minute preparations for the festivities. This year, however, everything had changed.

Lisa rose early to de-ice her car, ready to be at the water's edge for 9am.

Heather and Clara watched from the window, commenting on the absurdity of someone having to scrape ice off their car to go and jump in the sea. It didn't compute for them, but Lisa wouldn't miss it.

Martha had sectioned off the afternoon for peeling potatoes and setting the dining table ready for her grown-up kids and their partners to arrive. But the first part of her Christmas Eve would be spent in the ocean.

Brydie and Kim, met on their street, donning Santa hats and changing robes, ready to walk with linked arms along to the slip. Their breath formed plumes of condensation as they chatted about all the chores they each had to do later that day.

Ray was already sitting on the wall of the slipway when they all arrived one by one. She was sipping mulled wine from a thermal travel mug and sporting flashing light-up reindeer antlers.

"Merry Christmas my favourite sea goddesses," she chimed as Brydie and Kim arrived, shortly followed by

Martha with her Christmas pudding beanie hat and Lisa in her tartan Santa hat.

"Are we insane?" Lisa asked, glancing at her watch. "The air temperature is one degree. It'll have to be a quick dip. Remember they say to only immerse yourself for as many minutes as there are degrees in the water."

"I'm perfectly happy with an in-then-out scenario," Martha replied. "I'm already chilly."

Kim was stomping on the frosty grass, enjoying the crunching sound as she shattered ice shards under her boots. She called out to the group, with a huge grin: "I can't believe we're dooking when there's ice on the ground. That's nuts." She stopped suddenly, and tiptoed quickly to her bag. "I have a little Christmas present for you all." She pulled out a stack of four small, flat, wrapped gifts and watched with excitement as they gently tore the tissue off, revealing small framed artworks, featuring five women from behind holding hands in the sea.

"Oh, Kim, they're gorgeous," Martha gushed and the others added compliments and thank yous.

Kim beamed. "I've started painting again. These were my first pieces, so I wanted you all to have them."

"That's really special," Brydie commented, flashing a look of pride deep into Kim's eyes. "Right. Shall we just go for it quickly?" she queried, taking the lead. "I've brought warm mince pies and hot chocolate for after."

"Excellent," Kim oozed.

They each stepped out of the safety of their thick robes, shuddering as the cold air snatched at their skin.

"Oh my god, I'm already freezing," Lisa said, through chattering teeth.

"I've got Ducky-thermometer-guy," Kim said, plopping him between her breasts for safety.

Wearing thick 5mm winter surf gloves and boots, they group walked down the slipway, grabbing on to each other for moral support. The cries of discomfort were more desperate at this time of year and a soundtrack of heavy breathing hissed rather loudly around the women.

"No Mike today?" Brydie asked, between sharp intakes of breath as she dealt with the shock on her skin.

Ray shook her head. "He says he'll come back in the water about March, which is fair enough. Anyway, it's nice to have it just the five of us. Like the early days." She beamed a cheery grin under the flashing lights display on top of her head as she splashed her arms with cold water and winced. "He's at his place waiting for a video call from his daughter, so that's nice."

"Ducky says four degrees," Kim announced. "Ho, ho, holy shit that's cold!"

"Jeepers, my fridge is four degrees!" Martha exclaimed.

"Keep moving ladies," Brydie advised, before plunging forward to start swimming. Her smile had disappeared as she focused on her movements and coping with the whole body intensity.

"Everything from the neck down hurts," Kim said, looking worried. "I feel a bit dizzy."

"Maybe you should get out," Ray suggested. "Have you eaten anything, or had a hot drink this morning?"

Kim shook her head. "No. I just legged it straight out of the house as soon as my mum arrived to watch the kids. I'll have breakfast when I go back."

"Maybe you should have started up your engines, if you know what I mean," Ray said. "You're maybe a bit depleted."

"I'm done," Lisa said, giving the group a big wave as she turned to make her way back to the slip. "I can't feel my fingers, even with these gloves on."

"Good call," Brydie said, reassuringly. "Go as soon as you feel the need. I've only got one more minute in me."

Kim perked up. "I'm feeling much better now," she said brightly. "Instead of pain, I've got that gorgeous tingly sensation. I almost feel warm."

Brydie frowned. "Don't stay in much longer. That's not necessarily a good sign."

Kim took off for a short stretch of breaststroke, leaving the group bobbing in a circle, discussing their pretend synchronised swimming team and which skimpy outfits they would wear for the upcoming championships. They settled on sequin bikinis and agreed they would begin their routine with a lobster claw hand movement in the centre of their circle.

"Then we can boost off each other's feet," Brydie suggested, pointing to Ray's floating feet. Ray understood loud and clear what Brydie wanted and pressed her surf boots against Brydie's allowing the pair to push away from each other, creating an enormous splash as their bodies were thrown backwards with the force. Laughter rang out across the water.

"We're going to win medals for this routine," Ray cheered.

Martha announced she was heading out to get changed and the others followed. All except Kim, who was swimming back to the group slowly.

"Are you coming out now?" Brydie called to her.

"Yeah," she responded. "You know me. I'm a slow swimmer."

The rest of the group were well underway with the complicated process of drying off with towels and contorting their bodies into clothing underneath their robes by the time Kim reached the slip. Her skin was bright red.

"Quick, get your towel round you and warm up," Brydie said urgently. "You were in longer than anyone else."

Kim exhaled. "It was exhilarating, wasn't it? I feel so zingy." She reached for her towel and began patting off the water droplets slowly, finding each dab of the towel stingy on her overly sensitive nerve endings as they reacted to the shock.

The others were now wrapped up in several layers, gloves and hats and sipping hot drinks, sitting on the wall. Kim was struggling to hold things as she began to shudder.

"I can't do up my zip," she stammered through chattering teeth. "My fingers aren't working."

Brydie stepped forward and helped her friend zip up. "Do this as quickly as you can," she said, with a slight warning tone. "I've never seen you like this."

Kim's jaw was bouncing as her body shook, causing her teeth to click together continually. She sat down on the wall, attempting to pull on her fleece-lined leggings, but her grip kept loosening and she kept dropping the trousers.

Brydie knelt on her towel on the ground and said: "Here, let me." She gently pulled Kim's trousers up past her knees then let Kim stand and finish the job. Then Brydie rummaged about in Kim's bag for her, passing her a T-shirt, then a hoodie. She pulled out a zip fleece from her own bag and handed it to Kim. "You need an extra layer today."

Kim was very quiet, her face solemn as she concentrated on tugging the clothing into place inside her baggy robe.

Eventually, when Kim was all pieced together, but still shaking violently, Brydie handed her a metal mug of hot chocolate. "Get this in you," she said warmly.

Kim could barely hold the mug, her hands were trembling so vigorously. She took the tiniest sips whenever she could steady herself enough.

"Eat," Brydie ordered caringly, as she held a still-warm mince pie up to Kim's mouth.

Being extremely compliant, Kim silently bit into the pie and nibbled it.

"I know what'll help everyone warm up," Martha said suddenly and ran to her car. She opened all the doors and switched on her stereo, blasting out Christmas Top Hits.

She had changed into a dry hat after the Christmas pudding hat got a soaking, and was now sporting a red, glitter cowboy hat with white fluffy trim. She began dancing around the car park next to the slip, waving her arms under the weight of her heavy changing robe and singing: "Snow is falling, all around me, children playing, having fun…"

Brydie let out a laugh as Ray and Lisa dashed to immediately join Martha on the concrete dance floor.

Brydie sat on the wall next to Kim, rubbing her shoulders and offering her more bites of warm pie as they both enjoyed the sight of their mad friends boogying and trying not to slip on slight frost patches.

Kim's face was pale as she turned to Brydie and said: "Let's dance. I think it'll help."

They joined the others, swaying and stomping around to the festive music, a smile slowly emerging on Kim's face as she got her blood flowing and the hot chocolate was beginning to thaw her core.

A dog walker, wrapped in a thick coat, gloves and hat

paused near the dancing women to wave his hands along to the music. They turned to reply with more waving and sang a few lines to him.

"Have you lot been in the water?" he called out over the music.

"Yep," Martha responded chirpily.

"You're absolutely bonkers," he replied with a laugh. "Well done ladies. And Merry Christmas!"

"Merry Christmas!" The Dookers responded as they danced by the sea in their array of headgear – an unusual sight to behold.

CHAPTER 31 – A YEAR OF DOOKING

In all weathers, at all times of day, the Brogie Bay Dookers had spent a full year embracing the Moray Firth together. To mark their anniversary, they were hosting The Mad Dookers' Sea Party. The only stipulation was mad hats in a sea theme.

It was a gorgeous, sunny May day – the best they'd seen in months, and potentially the best they'd see for the rest of the year. There were always jokes in this part of the world that "summer fell on a Wednesday this year" and such like. When you get a hot day in northern Scotland you appreciate the hell out of it, as it may be a while until another one comes along.

The grass next to the slipway was a hive of activity as people settled on picnic blankets and camp chairs around a run of folding tables, which were laden with enough food to rival a medieval banquet.

"Watch out," Ray called out, as she placed a huge, lidded pot on one of the tables. "This one's hot. It's Thai red curry and rice."

Brydie's eyebrows shot up. "Wow. I just brought crisps. I wasn't expecting anyone to cook a whole meal."

Martha was busy inflating unicorn drinks holders and dishing them out to the group, while Kim was popping bottles of prosecco and pouring the golden liquid into paper cups.

Doug lay back on a picnic blanket, allowing the sun's

warmth to wash over him, while Lucas and Millie were playing in the shallow water off the slipway with their new body boards.

Kim's two – Stan and Gigi – had buckets and were up to their knees at the rocks looking for sea creatures.

Lisa and Heather were sipping beers in camp chairs, enjoying the freedom of being able to wear only T-shirts and get some vitamin D on their skin from the sun.

Mike and Ron were by the picnic table, munching on treats and discussing their tactics for just 'braving it out' when their balls would inevitably react to the chill of the water. Ron was a newbie, so Mike was his moral support. "We'd better warn Doug, too," Mike said, thinking of his fellow male.

Kim threw her summer dress to the ground, revealing her swimsuit and placed a latex dolphin head on her own head. "I can barely see! Who's coming in?"

A recently tattooed mermaid sat proudly on her right thigh, like a flag representing her sea swimming pride.

The Dookers grabbed their costumes and dashed towards her. Ray was a pirate, Martha was a lobster, pulling on a full body suit complete with lobster tail at the knees and a hat with eyes on it. Brydie was a mermaid with a tiara made from shells and pearls and Lisa had a large foam octopus on a headband. She kept having to bat the legs away from her eyes. Heather was joining the group for her first swim, wearing blue gems along her cheekbones and a toy seagull tied onto her hair bun.

The hardened Dookers showed very little reaction to the water temperature, as this was the warmest they'd felt the sea for about six months. The only gasps and yelps that could be heard were from the new swimmers. Doug ran into the water, barely giving himself a chance to feel shock, wearing a fishing captain's cap, prompting a chorus of "aye aye captains" from everyone around.

Brydie leapt onto Kim's back, who proceeded to walk around, still sporting the dolphin head. As she was carried around in piggyback mode, Brydie called out triumphantly: "I've always wanted to ride on a dolphin. This is a dream come true!"

Martha raised her paper cup in Brydie's direction and declared "Cheers to you!"

This corner of the ocean was alive with celebration and sunshine. It was the perfect way to end one year, as well as to launch a new year, of dooking.

"Cannonball!" came a cry from up on the wall which ran alongside the water. The group looked up just in time to see Clara and Rebecca leap off the wall and plummet into the water, causing two enormous splashes which sent light ripples of waves towards the Dookers.

Lisa was astounded. "Nice one, girls!" she shouted to her daughter and friend once they'd resurfaced. She turned to Heather with an emotional smile. They didn't need to say a thing. Their smiles said it all. Acceptance and happiness had found their girl.

It was 365 days since the first group swim and look how far they had all come. As if to mark this moment for them, a pod of local dolphins swam by, gently gliding along the top of the water to show off their fins.

"Did you organise this?" Doug whispered to Brydie with a wink, as he put his arm around her below water.

"Of course I did," she teased.

Everyone stood quietly in the water, watching the magnificent creatures, as if they were standing to attention in the presence of their ocean leaders.

It was rare for the Dookers to be so quiet, but

sometimes, even *they* were still stunned into awe in this magical part of their village by the sea. Their connection with the water – and each other – was deeper than ever.

THE END

Printed in Great Britain
by Amazon

42118190R00138